Silver Cloud was a bad-luck horse. Or so they said. But Jim Walker could not bring himself to believe this, despite the fact that the Mexican who had brought the stallion to the Purple Mountains country had been mysteriously murdered just after he had sold the horse, and the owner had died after being smashed up by Silver Cloud. Now Jim had the magnificent stallion—won when Bart Dodge foolishly told him he could keep Silver Cloud if he could stay on his back. Now Dodge regretted this impetuous move, was after the stallion, and would not rest until he had gotten it back . . .

THE SILVER STALLION

Fred N. Kimmel

Curley Publishing, Inc.
South Yarmouth, Ma.

Library of Congress Cataloging-in-Publication Data

Kimmel, Fred N.
   The silver stallion / Fred Kimmel.
      p.   cm.
   1. Large type books.   I. Title.
   [PS3561.I422S57   1992]
   813'.54—dc20
   ISBN 0–7927–1231–5 (hardcover lg. print)   91–31630
   ISBN 0–7927–1232–3 (softcover lg. print)   CIP

Published in Large Print by arrangement with Donald Mac-Campbell, Inc. in the United States and Canada.

Printed in Great Britain

CHAPTER ONE

Jim Walker, a gunnysack of food tied to the saddle horn, was heading his mustang toward the brakes of the Purple Mountains when he heard the uproar from the livery stable corral at the lower end of the town's one dusty street. As the shouts continued, he drew rein, his curiously light blue-gray eyes alive with interest. It was not yet noon; he could afford a few minutes to see what was going on back there and still make the long ride home, arriving before deep dark. Besides, he only made the trip from his remote cabin about four times a year when supplies ran low. He neck-reined the mustang around and rode back down the street at a walk.

Walker knew few people in the town of Purple, partially because his visits were so infrequent, but largely because the lonely years behind him had taught him bitterly that few people were worthy of a man's trust. At his remote cabin, his companions were his mustang, a mule and a few head of cattle. They were company enough.

At about twenty-six, he stood slightly more than six feet and weighed a hard hundred and eighty pounds. His browned features were clearly defined, except for the slight bulge at the

1

bridge of his nose. His cheekbones were sharp and high, almost aboriginal, and his eyes were a light shade of blue-gray, tending toward silver.

Of all his physical characteristics, it was his eyes that made men leave him alone. At times they shimmered in their extreme lightness, and took on a wild look, such as one sees in the eyes of animals in the dark. He had never packed a gun while in Purple, at least none that the inhabitants could see. However, in that little cattle town, the apparent absence of a weapon did not necessarily mean that a person was unarmed. He wore his habitual blue denim, clean but patched and sewn in a thousand and one places, and the soft cowhide boots that covered his feet were scratched and run-over at the heels.

Jim rode up to the fence corral. About twenty men were roosting on the high top rail, whooping and cheering as a cursing, dust-encrusted cowboy was scrambling up the rails from the inside. He was hatless, his eyes wide, frightened.

Inside the ring of boards was a sight to take away a man's breath. A huge stallion was walking across the arena on his mighty-thewed hind legs, his forefeet pawing the air like a boxer. His mane, which caught the sunlight and shone silver, flew erect at each jolting step. His neck was arched, his ears pricked high and alert. From his curled lips came a wild, defiant

2

trumpeting as he approached the bars. Those onlookers near him hastily clambered down to the safety of the outside.

Jim dropped from the saddle, leaving the reins to trail, and stood spellbound at sight of this magnificent horse. Now the great animal dropped his forehoofs and, noticing the men had disappeared from the fence, stared about to see from which direction his tormentors would next come at him. He wore a double bridle curb and a snaffle bit, but his antics had snapped the martingale and it dangled loosely from his chest. The saddle was in place, but the stirrups were popping viciously. He attempted to shuck the maddening leather by rolling in the dust and scraping it off on the ground.

The horse had a brown sheen on his lower parts that turned to a soft silver above the fetlocks. Just above the wild, rolling eyes, his face was marked by a diamond blaze, the lower point of which trailed down his nose in a thin streak of white. His ears were small, sharp and pointed, and a bang of silver mane flopped foolishly between them. His huge nostrils were flaring with rage.

Jim stepped up to the corral and climbed to the top. He had eyes only for the horse and he paid no attention to the looks of amusement in the faces of the others. He knew that his ragged appearance had been a topic of conversation before this among the citizens of Purple. He was used to it and knew that the surest way to a peaceful life was to disregard some things. It was not his nature, however, to overlook anything like the beautiful horse before him.

Now the horse backed off a few paces, staring at the newest encroacher on the edge of the fence. A hush fell as those on the opposite side and those who had dropped to the ground watched to see what the horse would do. He surprised them by ignoring the newcomer and circling inside the corral at a prancing run, his neck arched proudly, his mane flying in the wind and his silver tail flying out behind him. Then he stopped and ran to the center of the corral, his deep blue eyes rolling and showing white as he awaited the next action on the part of his two-legged enemies. He stood perfectly still with one leg slightly forward, his tail switching slowly.

Pop Holt, proprietor of the livery stable, climbed to the top bar of the corral near Jim and let fly a long spurt of tobacco juice into the enclosure. He was one of the few people in the town aside from Morton, the storekeeper, to whom Walker ever spoke. His silver-stubbled countenance sparkled in the sun and he grinned, showing tobacco-stained teeth.

Walker said: 'What's the big fellow's monicker?' He nodded toward the horse.

'Why, that's Silver Cloud. Walker, you mean you ain't heerd tell o' him yet? Belongs to Cap

4

Dodge, over there.' Pop spat in the direction of a man on the other side of the fence.

Jim glanced up, his brow clouded. He should have known that the beautiful animal would belong to Bart Dodge, who owned everything that was any good in the Purple Valley. His glance fell short of the owner of Purple Valley's biggest ranch, the Pitchfork. He looked back at the horse.

'How old is he?' asked Jim.

'Three years, an' never been rode. Jes' come to town fer a new set o' shoes. He's all shoed up now and feelin' his oats. Some hoss, ain't he?'

'Silver Cloud's the right name for him,' Jim answered, and looked off into the clouds that hung against the backdrop of the Purples.

The cowboy who had left the corral so hastily was the foreman of Pitchfork, Dodge's ranch. His name, Walker knew, was Lash Wade. Lash was swatting the dust from his clothes and cursing the stallion. He limped off toward a group of men on the far side of the corral that surrounded Dodge. The whoops of derision of the cowboys caused him to color red beneath his deep tan. Even Captain Dodge was laughing.

'Who wants a try at it?' shouted Dodge. He was a handsome, vain man who never could bear to be far from the center of the stage. More than anything else he loved the deep, rich tones of his own baritone voice, which usually

5

silenced all others in any argument.

'I'll try it,' shouted a thin cowboy.

There was a laugh from the crowd.

'You've tried for two years now, Craig Briggs. What makes you think you can make it this time?' laughed Dodge.

'I think I can ride him today,' insisted Briggs.

'You can't, though,' asserted Dodge, and the finality of his tone made everyone aware that Briggs would not touch the leather on Silver Cloud.

Jim gritted his teeth. He hated Dodge for making fun of the thin cowhand who was good enough to ride in all weather for the Pitchfork brand but not good enough to participate in a little sport that might bring him some small fame. Walker glanced at Dodge, deciding that the owner probably didn't want the horse ridden. No doubt Dodge enjoyed the glory of owning such a horse—an animal that no one could ride.

It was a shame, Jim reflected, that the horse couldn't be broke. He had seen similar horses in his travels, and he knew that a horse allowed to go on like this would get worse every year and might even turn killer. Once that happened, its usefulness to man would be over. He was half-tempted to ride the horse himself. He was a good rider and possessed a way with animals, but he knew that Dodge wouldn't let

6

him near the stallion.

Old Pop Holt, hunched on the top rail beside him, broke the sudden quiet by saying, 'Whyn't let young Walker, here, give Cloud a ride?'

Jim felt the color rise in his face, and he stared down at the dust. If Dodge wouldn't let one of his own riders try the horse, then he was surely out. Besides, he didn't relish the lameness that a tough bucking horse would put onto his bones.

'Who the hell is Walker?' roared Dodge.

Somebody near him muttered something and Jim glanced up, anger suddenly welling within him, wishing he had caught the comment. Dodge knew full well who he was, it was just his galling, overbearing manner. Now the rancher glanced across the corral, his eyes sparkling.

'Oh, *that* Walker,' he remarked. 'How about it, Walker—think you could ride Silver Cloud?'

He voiced his query in such a way as to cause laughter, and made it seem more of an insult than a question. Jim spat into the dust. He told himself to climb off the corral and get on his mustang; no good could come from riding Dodge's horse or from even trying. But something stubborn within him made him answer:

'Yeah, I reckon I could stay on that horse. I reckon any *man* could.' As he expected, the comment brought some dark looks but there

7

were none as stormy as that on the rancher's face.

He glowered back at Jim. 'If you ride that horse, Walker—you can have him!'

There was a gasp from the crowd. A full twenty witnesses heard the remark and, considering the horse, it was a wild one. The men looked at one another.

Jim's heart quickened as he looked at the silver and brown animal. Quickly he stepped down into the corral.

Morton, the storekeeper, looked at Dodge and spoke: 'Listen, Bart, I hope you know what you just said—that you'll *give* Jim, here, the horse if he rides him. Is that right?'

'He *can't* ride him,' Dodge said contemptuously. He was angry at having made the reckless remark, but to back water even on that small a point was something his pride couldn't allow. He could see the cowboys staring at him and he bit his lip when the thought came that the wild-looking Walker just might ride the horse. No; that was impossible, he decided. No man in the valley could ride the horse, and the best riders rode for his Pitchfork brand. Walker had about one chance in a million to stay on the horse. There was no time limit; the rider would have to stay aboard until the horse stopped to blow. No, the rancher decided, there was no chance that this hillbilly cowboy could do it.

8

'But if he does, then he keeps the horse—that's what you said,' Morton reminded him.

Damn the man, thought Dodge. There was animosity between the storekeeper and himself ever since his bill had become so large. Morton was constantly after him to lower the running balance, having the nerve to point out that the rancher could spend less on other things and keep his store bill lower. Dodge wished Morton hadn't been there.

'All right—isn't that what I said?' asked Dodge. He turned to the others. It was better to reaffirm it than to back out, and anyway Walker would never be able to ride the horse. The men around him started to smile and nod. Money was bet as Jim walked after the slowly retreating horse, talking soothingly and watching for a chance to catch the reins and vault into the saddle.

CHAPTER TWO

A wild gladness rose in Walker as he went after the horse. He knew that when the other riders had mounted him, several of Dodge's hands must have tossed loops over the animal's neck to hold him down from different directions. Walker knew he would have to gain the saddle the hard way; but as his eyes lovingly noted the points of the horse, he didn't care. All he had to do was to catch up the reins and get in the saddle, then if he could stay in the saddle, the horse was his. Dodge had spoken before a score of witnesses and the man was too proud to go back on his word.

Laughter from the others as well as that from the handsome Bart Dodge rang in his ears as the horse evaded him in the enclosure. No matter how he circled or approached, the horse always trotted out of his reach, the ends of the loose reins flying near the flashing, sharp hoofs. Nobody offered the use of a rope, so Jim started toward the edge of the corral to get his own.

As he put his foot on the bottom board the horse reared again and, dropping down, bent his knees and rolled, trying to dislodge the saddle. Walker whirled and raced across the corral like a shot, his sudden, unexpected movement astounding the fence riders. He hit the saddle at the precise moment that Silver Cloud stiffened his forefeet to stand. One of the free reins Walker snatched on his way past the startled horse's head and once in the saddle he leaned around the animal's neck and gathered the loose leather.

Silver Cloud snorted with rage; he had rolled on the ground to rid himself of the cursed saddle, and now a man had taken advantage of it to mount his back once more. The horse struggled up on his hind legs under the added burden of the rider and stood spread-legged, nostrils flaring, sides heaving. The sight brought a gasp from the crowd that had never seen him stand as still as this with a rider on his back.

Jim settled himself tightly in the saddle and jabbed the horse gently with his heels. Silver Cloud arched his neck slowly, shuddering as he did so. Then he lowered his head and the crowd began to jabber excitedly. Bart Dodge, seething with rage, sat on the edge of the corral, deaf to the conversation of those around him.

Then the horse suddenly skyrocketed and the cowboys whooped with delight. The animal's action startled everyone except Walker who had felt something building up inside the horse between his legs. So he had been ready for the back-arching leap into the sky.

But the descent was another thing. Straight down the horse plummeted, legs stiffly extended. As each hoof slammed into the ground the impact was transmitted to the rider in separate, bone-rattling jars. Walker felt his hat fly free, then his chin crashed against his chest and he felt a tooth puncture the inside of his lip.

No sooner was he down than up into the sky again went Silver Cloud and Walker could see why the horse was so named. Once more came the jarring shock of hoofs hitting the ground,

11

with Walker's stomach staying somewhere above his throat. A blinding flash of pain shot across his eyes, then man and horse were again in dizzying flight. Sickened, Jim caught the blur of faces along the rail.

Once he saw the gleeful face of Dodge just as he lost a stirrup. He knew that one more leap would throw him. But the horse fell to bucking his rear legs and Jim retrieved the stirrup and stiffened himself against the jolting, excruciating agony.

Around the corral the horse flew, frogwalking one minute, trying to sunfish the next. Then Jim jerked his leg back with a cry of pain as the horse twisted his head around and sank his teeth into the rider's calf. The animal felt him lose control and at once skyrocketed, throwing Jim forward over the pommel and astraddle the horse's neck.

To those watching, it seemed that Jim's ride was finished, but the next moment a jolt somehow threw him backward into the saddle. The stirrups were now lost and flopping wildly, but he dug his heels in under Silver Cloud's belly and prayed for a miracle. One of the reins was lost and he could only partially curb the animal with the other, while his free hand clutched the saddle horn. He could see the glistening foam fly from the horse's mouth; he could feel him start to tire. The saddle was treacherously slippery with sweat and as the horse pitched violently to the side Jim started to slip out. Barely conscious, Jim hung on by sheer blind instinct as he slipped and slid in the wet seat. What was more, he no longer cared about riding the horse or owning it.

Then it happened. The horse went down on one side and started to roll. Jim's foot touched the ground and he stepped clear. He could not hear the shouts of encouragement or advice. Still holding one rein, he ran around the downed horse that was thrashing up clouds of dust so thick that those on the fence could scarcely tell man from horse. He looped the rein over the horse's head and circled the animal, grabbing by guess for the loose rein and coming up with it in the dust. And as Silver Cloud started up again, Walker was back in the saddle. When the forelegs of the animal stiffened, Walker's feet were on the stirrup bars.

His head rose out of the dust above that of the horse and there was a glad yell from the crowd. Silver Cloud shot out of the dust and, being lashed with the loose rein-ends and spurred hard, ran in a circle that saw him do more carrying and less bucking that he had ever done.

The horse wasn't yet through; he had other tricks for a rider who stuck this long. Now he headed for the rough boards of the fence and went scraping along them. Walker met this

13

tactic by lifting his near leg and hooking it safely over the saddle horn. In retaliation, he spurred and reined the horse against one of the upright corral poles, a hide-bruising experience that took Silver Cloud off guard. Twice more he rolled; after the second time he found the rider back in the saddle the instant he tried to rise, he came slowly to his feet. He was blowing, and was through for the day. He stood stock-still in the afternoon sun and lowered his head.

Jim held the saddle. His clothes were ripped, he dripped sweat and was mud-caked from rolling in dust. His hands, face, arms and legs were scratched and bruised. His nose was bleeding and he had a smile on his face. The sweat-covered horse didn't move as Walker stepped down and walked to the corral gate. He left it open, walked to his own mustang and started to untie the thong on his rope.

From the corner of his eye he saw Bart Dodge come toward him, but he pretended not to notice. Suddenly the whoops and shouts of a moment before turned to whispers as the cowboys, breaking into little groups, speculated on Walker's ride and the promise Dodge had foolishly given.

Dodge was coming rapidly toward him, his face dark and truculent. A small knot of men walked in his wake, among them, his foreman, Lash Wade. Morton was coming along in the rear, slightly separated from the group.

14

Still pretending not to see them, Jim turned away, giving the approaching party his back, and started for the corral with his coiled rope.

'Just a minute, Walker! Where you think you're goin'?' asked Dodge, his voice touched with anger.

'Goin' to get my horse!' answered Jim, without turning.

Dodge ran a few steps forward and grabbed him by the arm. Jim was amazed at the power in the man's hand that halted him instantly. He whirled, trying to keep the pain from showing in his face, and struck with the coiled rope at the big rancher's wrist. Dodge grinned as the rawhide folded harshly about his arm but maintained his grip. Their eyes locked and, as Dodge tried to return Walker's cold stare, he relaxed his grip and a smile came to his lips.

'You didn't think I was *serious*, did you, Walker? How could you think for a minute that just riding that horse makes him yours?'

'Let go my arm, Dodge!' said Walker, his voice soft.

'Of course. Come now, fella, surely you recognize that my saying I would give you the horse was only a figure of speech. Why, a man would be a fool to give away a horse like that, and he's twice as valuable now that he's been ridden.' Dodge was becoming alarmed; he wanted to play a heavier hand but others were watching and he dared not go too far. He

15

struggled to control himself.

'The horse is a gift to me if I ride him—that's how I interpret what you said.'

Walker glanced at the men behind Dodge, all hired hands of the ranch owner. 'Isn't that the way you fellows heard it?'

The suddenness of the question caught them off guard and they looked abashed at one another, keeping silent for fear of saying the wrong thing. They were all hard and lean, used to getting the short end of things themselves, and Walker counted that they would recognize in him one of their own kind and at least say nothing against him. He was right about that.

'These fellows have nothing to say about it, Walker. This horse is my property, not theirs. Now, as for the ride, I'll pay you what you think it's worth. How about ten dollars?'

In spite of Dodge's welching on the promise, the offer brought some approving nods from the men gathered around the pair. After all, ten dollars in days when a man worked for thirty a month was a third of a month's wages.

Walker shook his head negatively and walked into the corral, closing the gate in the faces of the group. Dodge flung open the gate angrily, striking one of those behind him, and strode inside. Jim walked right up to the horse and removed the cruel bit, throwing it into the dust. Then he stepped around to the side of the horse and stripped off the saddle and blanket. Dodge

16

regarded him angrily. Jim took the least sweaty side of the blanket and began to wipe the horse with it. His air was calm, and he talked softly to the horse as he worked. The animal raised his head and pricked his ears alert.

'What you think you're doin'?' demanded Dodge.

'I'm rubbin' him down best I can,' declared Jim.

'Why'd you throw my bridle on the ground?'

"Cause that's your bridle and this is my horse, Mister Dodge. That's no fit bridle for a horse, anyhow. Look how his mouth is bleedin'!'

Walker, finished with the brief rubdown, picked up his rawhide rope and began to work the line into a crude hackamore which he looped over the horse's ears and down beneath the hinge of his jaw and thence around the nose.

Lash Wade stepped forward. 'The boss was just kiddin', Walker, when he said you could have the hoss. Everybody knows that but you, you dumb-lookin' fool. Why you can't get it through your thick head is more than I can figure out. Now give me that there rope an' stand aside while I hitch Silver Cloud to the back of our wagon.'

Lash stepped forward and reached for the rope, but Walker held it away from him. Wade stared into the eyes of the loner and what he saw made him hold back. What it was he wasn't sure, but it looked as if Jim Walker was laughing at him or had some secret that he, Lash Wade, didn't know about. Wade hitched up his pants, wondering if Walker wore a gun. Walker was a good twenty pounds under his own weight and he judged he could take him in a fight; still there was the fact that Walker had ridden the horse and he had failed repeatedly.

'Why, I was the one that tuckered that hoss,' Wade said. He continued, 'I got Silver Cloud winded and then you step aboard and claim all the credit, eh?'

'Just a minute, Wade,' the storekeeper's neutral voice cut through. The middle-aged man with the gray muttonchop sideburns stepped through the crowd. 'Walker, here, made a good ride and there ain't no one here today, leastwise none that calls himself a man, that will deny it. I see him break the horse and so did you. Now Bart made the deal, it was his own doin' and I never knowed him to back out. Unless he buys the horse back, I'd say that the horse belongs to Walker.'

Jim didn't look at the storekeeper but in his heart he thanked the man who seemed his only friend in the ever-tightening circle around himself and the exhausted horse. News of the ride had leaked out and people were coming from everywhere to join the crowd, making it impossible for him to lead out the horse.

'All right,' Dodge said. 'I made the statement

18

and it was a slip of the tongue. I'm big enough to admit I let my lip flap once too often, and it's a good lesson for me.' He turned to the others and smiled good-naturedly, getting answering grins in return. 'How many times have one of you made some fool statement that just don't hold any meaning? This was one of them. I was disgusted with the horse at the time and I said a stupid thing, but there was no serious legal agreement made to transfer the horse to this man.' He nodded toward Jim Walker.

Walker stood silently holding the rope close to the hackamore he had fashioned and stroking the horse's nose. He felt a smoldering hate growing within himself. Dodge was winning the crowd over to his side; he was making each of them feel in his place—as though every man there had made the stupid statement and then was dutybound to stand behind it. The men could see the rancher's point and Walker felt the crowd's sudden animosity.

A moment before he had been a sort of hero to them but now they were beginning to look at him as a fool for thinking he had any claim to the horse. After all, he was nothing but a ragged, lone wolf down from a scrub ranch in the brakes. What right did a character like him have to a horse like Silver Cloud? Only men like Bart Dodge—strong, handsome and dashing—should ride thoroughbreds. Why didn't he take the ten dollars Dodge had generously

19

offered—that was good money for one ride. Now Dodge took the conversation again.

'Since Walker now owns the horse on the barest of technicalities—which, I might add, would never stand up in any court of the land—I'll do the sporting thing and pay him a good price for the animal.'

The remark brought a cheer from the crowd, which was now completely in Dodge's corner.

Walker had dreaded any such announcement. In his own mind he was beginning to doubt that he really had any claim to the horse. He feared refusing a cash offer in front of the crowd. Above all, he hated being in the center of things like this, whereas he could see that Bart Dodge was in his element, holding the center of the stage. In between his remarks about the horse, he easily carried on four or five conversations at once with people who were eager to speak with him.

'The horse is not for sale,' declared Jim flatly as he tightened his fist on the rope. He was almost ashamed of the way his voice sounded. He always had difficulty talking before a crowd and his remark sounded in his ears like the hastily interjected comment of a schoolboy trying to make himself heard. Several people laughed as he said it.

Dodge turned, grinning triumphantly. 'Hear that, folks? Walker says the horse isn't for sale.' He burst out laughing and the crowd eagerly joined him.

Morton had stepped close to Walker's ears and whispered, 'If he makes an offer, you'd better take it and skedaddle, son.'

Dodge turned back toward Jim, holding his wallet with one hand and counting out bills with the other. 'All right, Mister Walker,' the rancher said. 'Here's fifty dollars, and you just give me a bill-of-sale—for my own horse. I've learned my lesson and from now on everything is going to be strictly legal.' He turned to the crowd and they laughed with him. Walker's lips started to move, and at first his words were lost in clamor. Then in silence they heard the last words: '—and I meant it, *no* amount of money can buy this horse. I aim to keep him. Now you all stand aside there. I'm coming through with the animal!'

'Just a minute, Walker,' demanded Dodge. There was a slight frown on his face but he hid it quickly. 'Here's a hundred dollars cash-money. Hand me that rope, like a good fellow.'

The generosity of this offer brought a good response from the onlookers. Walker felt like a fool for not taking it; the hundred dollars would buy the bull he wanted, plus a new stove for his shack. Still, the beautiful horse meant more to him, and under its coating of dust his face turned a deeper shade of red. Now he was in a worse spot than ever and he angrily determined to be stubborn and keep the horse. Dodge, who had welched on his promise, was making himself look like the injured one to the crowd.

'Take it, son,' advised Morton in a loud tone. 'He's giving you a good deal, considerin' everything.' Jim could see that even the storekeeper was quickly losing interest in his cause.

'A thousand dollars wouldn't be enough. All right, stand clear—*Heeeyah!*' Walker dropped several coils of the rope and with the loose end slapped the horse through the gathering. Shouting in alarm, they fell back as Silver Cloud burst forward on the end of the rope.

CHAPTER THREE

'Grab the fool and take the horse from him,' shouted someone. A man put his hand on Jim's sleeve as he passed through the gap left by the advancing horse. Walker jerked his arm and lashed out with the loose end of the rawhide rope. The crowd split back with those in the front stepping on the feet of those behind them and drawing their curses.

Behind Jim, Lash Wade dropped his hand to the butt of his Colt but Dodge intercepted his draw with a frown and staying motion of his hand. No one in the crowd noticed the movement as they were all scrambling out of the way of the horse and its new owner.

Walker climbed into the mustang's saddle and tied the free end of the rope to the saddle horn. He rode out of town at a half-trot, his body straight in the saddle, followed by admiring and awesome glances from the crowd. Dodge's crew headed for the saloon with Bart and Lash following, talking earnestly between themselves.

Walker took the valley road, keeping the horse at the half-trot until he was well clear of town, then rode at an easier pace. Well into the valley he swung off the road and, using the tallest peak of the Purples for a steering point, moved across the open land. He passed to the south of Dodge's Pitchfork, then made the turn around the stand of lodgepole pine that sheltered the Ackerman place. Smoke rose from its chimney.

Now he angled for the brakes. His own shack was out of sight but he stared ahead at the place where he knew it nestled among the pines and rocks. It was just a one-room cabin with heavy log walls; outside he had a pole corral and a dug well lined with rock. There was a small garden for fresh vegetables in the growing season; the rest of the year he lived on what his gun could bring down in the foothills, and occasionally he butchered one of his own cattle.

It was almost dark when he reached the

forlorn-looking place, made even more lonely now by the long shadows of the Purples. He turned the horses into the corral, then before entering the shack he went around to the shed in back and brought a few forksful of hay around for the horses and the mule. He grained them next, giving the stallion an extra bait of barley as a token of friendship. Still not believing that he owned the animal, he stood awhile watching him pace the corral before he shouldered the sack and went inside.

Jim struck a match and lighted the kerosene lamp, bringing the room alive with the soft yellow light. He sniffed of the kerosene on his fingers and wiped them on the back of his pants. Next he built up a fire in the stove, an old sheet-iron army model that had seen better days but it would hold coals for a good spell and it was good enough for him.

The furniture, a bed, several straight chairs, a table, and one big frame-and-cowhide chair, was all solid stuff that he had made himself. He went about transferring the things he had bought into battered storage tins. Last of all, he brought forth a can of peaches and set it carefully on the shelf. He did not need the peaches and he could not afford such luxuries, but the picture on the label had been so beautiful he had fairly drooled while looking at it in the store. He promised himself he would savor its sight for a few days before opening the can.

The coffeepot was soon boiling and hissing on the stove with the pungent aroma filling the cabin. He fried up a big panful of bacon and beans and baked a biscuit in a small tin oven perched precariously on the side of the stove top. He washed down the solitary meal with frequent cups of coffee. After eating, he cleaned the dishes and refilled the stove with a fresh supply of wood. As the sides of the metal turned to a rosy glow he packed tobacco into his pipe and, propping his feet on a box, leafed through his battered copy of *Don Quixote* until he found his place.

Walker read a few pages and fell asleep, his tired body aching with pain and welcoming the idleness, the warmth of the stove. He slept deep and well. It was not unusual for him to sleep in the chair until morning. He dreamed about Bart Dodge and Silver Cloud; once he awoke for a second, thinking he had heard the shrill whicker of one of the horses, but quickly went back to sleep when no further noises came from outside.

The first shafts of sunlight came down through the Purple Valley, striking the rocks that were moist and glistening with dew, invading the brakes where it could find passage through the treacherous country. Inside his cabin, Walker stirred slowly, rubbing at his mouth with a bruised and scratched hand. He began to stretch, then remembering the stallion, he suddenly bounded out of the chair and raced to the door, eager for his first morning glimpse of the animal in his own corral.

He thrust open the door and stared at the corral, scarcely believing his eyes. Except for the mule, which never would wander far from the grain box, the corral was empty. Both the mustang and Silver Cloud were gone.

Shouting an oath, Walker dashed into the yard and looked around. There were boot tracks at the corral and the bars had been let down by those who had made the tracks. Jim ignored the tracks and started to saddle the mule. He didn't have to be an expert tracker to guess who would be likely to steal the horse.

He started to swing into the saddle and then hesitated. Stepping down, he then headed for the house, shaking his head, a sad look on his face. Inside, he tossed some tattered, torn newspapers and magazines from the top of the chest at the foot of his bed. He opened the chest and brought forth a holstered Colt and shell belt.

Walker buckled on the gun. While most of Jim Walker's earthly possessions were of the battered, secondhand variety, the Colt was an outstanding exception; it was a late model and well cared for. A blue-steel weapon, it had smooth mother-of-pearl handles. The trigger guard was of polished brass. Even the holster was of oiled cowhide, smooth, dark leather without a single scuffmark. The gun glided in and out of the leather easily as Walker tried it several times, then he flashed it forth in a blur of movement and dropped it back into place again.

The gun looked unused except for the places where the bluing was burned away near the cylinder ports by the searing flashes of hundreds of explosions. He stopped at the shelf and dipped out a pocketful of .45 shells from the can where he stored his extras. Then he went out and climbed onto the mule.

He moved away at a fast walk with the saddle creaking and harness jingling in the fresh morning air. He passed the place where the horsemen had dismounted and had stolen up on the corral. The tracks were confused by the horses' hoofmarks overlapping one another on the trail, but Walker knew there had been at least six riders and this made him laugh grimly. Bart Dodge might as well have left his signature, for six riders was a force that no one else in the valley could afford to send. Of course, Walker realized that it would be almost impossible to prove that Dodge's men had taken the animal. They could hide out the stallion in some remote canyon and Jim could look for months without ever seeing Silver Cloud. In nearly lawless Purple Valley, possession was truly nine points of the law and the rugged settlers had little respect for those who could not hold onto their own.

Out here, there would be no one like the storekeeper, Morton, to come to his aid; these people took care of their own fights and stayed out of those of others. Everyone in the valley thought of Jim Walker as a loner, anyway, and he was avoided whenever possible. Naturally, living alone on the edge of the treacherous brakes country, he was suspect every time a steer turned up missing or found butchered.

The brakes were shunned by most of the ranchers as a menace to their cattle; it was expensive to haze stock out of the rough country and easy to lose them altogether and have them go wild. Wild steers were further trouble because they came down out of the brakes at night and ran off cows from the branded herds. Also the brakes were traditionally regarded as the hiding place of rustlers and outlaws who crossed the Purples and camped in the conveniently wild country of the brakes. Occasionally, their fires could be seen on clear nights when they camped there before moving on to new territory. Anyone who lived close to the brakes was branded in the minds of cow-people as at least semi-renegades, if not worse.

Purposely he swung closer to the Ackerman place than was his usual habit. He didn't suspect them and yet he was so inflamed over losing the stallion that he wanted a look at their corral even if from a distance. He saw old Ackerman out near the corral, gazing at some horse stock. The animals were too bunched to see if the stallion was among them, so Jim slanted toward the yard.

A girl came out with a basket of wash, and he knew that she alone was the reason he didn't suspect Ackerman. The old man's daughter Sally was beautiful and he didn't want to think that the father of such a girl would steal anything. He came quickly into the yard. Although the mule had a brisk walk, he surmised he must look ridiculous on the long-eared animal. He wished he could have ridden in on the stallion instead, then perhaps the girl would have given him more than a passing glance before going back to hanging the wash.

He had never paid them a visit in the last two years, and he realized that now he wouldn't even recognize their voices. A few times they had waved at him when he was riding to his shack, or when the old man was up in the high country he would sometimes yell hello from a distance. They were the kind of neighbors that Jim Walker liked. They let him alone, and this was fine for a man who wanted to keep people and things at a good distance.

CHAPTER FOUR

Old Dan Ackerman stepped down from the corral where he had been standing on the lower bars. He was in his fifties with snowy hair and brown leather skin, his face deeply seamed. A triangular swatch of white hair showed on his brow, escaping from under his Stetson brim. His throat was wrinkled where his collar was open at the neck of his blue checked shirt. He wore a pair of faded Levi's tucked into his boot tops, and his hands were jammed into his rear pockets. He glanced at Walker who was looking at the horses in the corral.

'Lookin' fer somethin', son?' he inquired.

'I'm lookin' for a horse. Some varmints stole him from my place last night—a big horse named Silver Cloud,' Jim answered.

'I already heard how you won him; Sally, over there, was in town yesterday,' Ackerman said, nodding toward the girl.

'Well, he ain't in there,' declared Jim, jerking the mule around.

'Hold on,' yelled Ackerman.

'Why?'

'Where you goin'?'

'None of your business where he's going, Dad,' interrupted the girl, walking toward them.

'Ain't, eh?' grumbled the old man.

'No, it isn't. If Mister Walker doesn't want to tell you where he's going, that's quite all right.' She smiled up at Walker on the mule.

Suddenly Jim wished he didn't have that scrubbly beard on his face. He nodded to her.

'Talkative son-of-a-gun, ain't he?' Ackerman asked dryly.

'Dad!' exclaimed the girl.

'Well, he ain't spoke to us in two years. Now he comes visitin' and says about ten words. I'll tell you one thing, son, if that Silver Cloud that you was fool enough to take away from Bart Dodge is gone this mornin', then you're plumb lucky. Ride home and say a few hally-loos and a couple of thank-Gods!'

'Why?'

'See what I mean?' said the old man. 'Regular talkin' fool, ain't he? "Why?" says he. Well I'll tell you why, 'cause you spend all your time up there in the brakes with your face hid behind a rock, so I gotta tell you what's goin' on in the world.'

'Don't pay any attention to him,' said the girl, smiling up at Walker.

Walker nodded.

Ackerman continued: 'That horse is pizen luck. Two yars ago that fancy Mexican brought him around here an' claimed he was an unbroke Appaloosy. The Mex said he was for sale, an' the biddin' started with ol' Colonel Randle and

Dodge goin' tooth an' nail. The Colonel had the cash an' he paid the Mex fifteen hundred dollars, silver. Dodge never forgive the Colonel for bringin' his cash to bear.

'The Mex lit out, but they found him at the foot of Glass Mountain where he was gettin' ready to cross the Purples. His throat was sliced from here to here!' His callused forefinger transcribed the course on his own neck. 'Colonel Randle, he had the damn hoss next an' he never could ride him, though he probably broke a half a thousand horses in his time around the valley. Finally the hoss broke ol' Randle's neck and he laid on his back a full nine months tryin' to live, until he got tired of it all and decided he'd lived long enough at seventy, anyhow.

'The Widder Randle, she had some sense. She sold that hoss to Bart Dodge fer five hundred dollars, paper. That was a thousand-dollar loss but it was the smartest move the old gal ever made. As soon as Dodge got that hoss, things started to go bad for him.' He finished his comments by an emphatic spit of tobacco juice into the dust, narrowly missing a wandering rooster.

'Why, Dad, that horse hasn't been bad luck to Bart,' declared the girl.

Jim Walker was surprised that the girl used Dodge's first name, but then she was good-looking and there was no reason why the

32

suave, eligible Dodge wouldn't be interested in her. And suddenly he had found another reason not to like the handsome rancher.

'Oh, he ain't bad luck, hey?' shouted her father. 'Well, I suppose it was good luck when the hoss kicked him last year and broke his arm? That's your idea of good luck, hey? An' how about when his hay went moldly on him in the rain last year, just after the hoss came to the ranch? Oh, I can tell you, Walker, that hoss has been nothin' but trouble for Dodge. Six men has been maimed by that hoss and two has lost their life by him, I swear. If I don't miss my guess, the Mex got killed because of that hoss. Don't get me wrong—I ain't wavin' my finger at Dodge—not that he ain't got the grit to kill, 'cause, by God, he has!'

'Dad!' exclaimed the girl, horrified.

'He has. I know what grit Dodge has in his craw, and by golly, I can see the same thing in this young feller's eyes. Pshaw, gal, you don't know, you ain't been around like I been around. Why, I saw Quantrill—saw him as close as I see you. Dodge's got the same look in his eyes, and so's this loner here—this talkin' fool, sittin' on a mule and listenin'. Some men talk, daughter, and some men don't talk and you gotta watch out for both kinds. One man can talk you plumb out o' your senses an' the other can silence you right out o' your heart. I don't know which is worse, to lose your sense or

33

to lose your heart, 'cause I ain't a cussed female. But you gotta watch out fer both—you mind me?'

'Oh!' declared the girl, her face turning red. She stalked back to the line where she was hanging the clothes.

'Where you goin', Talkative?' Ackerman said.

'Only one place to go—Dodge's camp,' declared Jim.

'How you know it was Dodge that pinched the stallion?'

'He sent six men.'

'Yeah, that was a fool stunt. He's got any one o' six that could steal a gent's watch, but he's about the only one that's got more than six riders to waste on a thing like this. What'll you do when you see your hoss over at his place?'

'Take him home.'

'Well, he ain't over to his place, of course. What kind of fool you think this Dodge is?'

'You know where the horse is?'

'I see them, all right, I see them,' winked the old man.

'When?'

'Oh, last night I heard the harness jingling. You know, in the old days we always muffled the harness with cloth so that it couldn't jingle, an' we even covered the hosses' shod hoofs with sacks so that they wouldn't sound on rock. Why, in the old days we could take a cavalry troop through a sleepin' Sioux village if we had a mind, an' not even the dogs would hear us. I heard them go jinglin' by last night on the way up to your place—got me out of bed, they did, with their damn noise. Passed right by the house, not a quarter mile off!'

Walker winced.

'Yessir,' continued Ackerman, 'I heard them go up, so I says, "I'll light up a pipe and watch 'em come down." I knew they was up to no good, you see. Pretty soon they come down, rattlin' like a potter's wagon, all laughin' and smokin' so that you could of seen them a mile off. I see the silver stallion too; they had him on a rope and he was sugar-footin' it along with a bag of oats over his nose. If you want to steal a hoss, just slip the oat bag over his nose. By God, those young fellows knew that trick, anyway. Well, getting back to the story, they headed for Dodge's line shack on the other side of the valley, over in the Cat Hills country. You can get there if you head straight across the valley from here. You probably won't find many guardin' him, either. Dodge don't keep many men in the Cat Hills; two-three at the most, sometimes only one.'

'Thanks,' smiled Walker. He reined the mule around and started to ride out of the yard.

'Wait!' shouted Ackerman.

'What is it?'

'I'll throw a saddle on the brindle there an'

hop along with you a piece. Who's gonna do your talkin'? You don't talk worth a damn.'

'I'll do my own talkin',' smiled Walker.

'With that Peacemaker, eh?' said Ackerman.

'Maybe,' Walker answered, the smile fading.

'Well, I'll ride over with you and do your talkin' for you, an' if I can't talk that Silver Cloud hoss into your pocket, you can shoot it in. Is that a deal?'

'Aren't you afraid of what Dodge will think?'

'Me afraid of Dodge? Why, I could spill ten drinks like him. Besides there's one thing in my favor—he's a mite sweet on Sally an' he ain't gonna do any sparkin' aroun' her, if he ever speaks unkindly to me. You hold that miserable mule while I drop a rope over that fool brindle's ears. I'd ride the zebra dun, but that's what that fool brindle expects me to do, an' I ain't lettin' no hoss outthink me!'

Ackerman stepped to the corral as Walker burst out laughing. Taking a coil of rope from around a post, he then shook out some coils and deftly tossed a loop over the head of the zebra dun who led the flow of circling horses around the corral. He snubbed the rope on the top bar, pulled the horse to the side of the fence and hitched him there. He walked to the shed and came out with blanket, saddle and bridle.

'You see, son,' Ackerman explained, 'that dun is so smart he understands man talk and I always have to fool him when I want him. If I

36

don't, he'll keep his head tucked into the middle o' the pack like it was a peach in a can. But this way, he thinks he's in no danger, and—bango!—I got him snagged.'

Ackerman went about saddling the horse with a good amount of cursing and yelling, and finally had the horse ready and out of the corral. Actually, Walker would have preferred that the old man stay at home, but his first close view of Sally had brought on a sudden desire to be friendlier with the Ackermans who were, after all, his neighbors. Perhaps the older man would help him to be cooler and do nothing that would disturb the peacefulness of his ranch in the brakes. Then, too, Ackerman knew the bigger part of Purple Valley and he could save time; the quicker he caught up with the stallion the better things would be.

Jim saw the girl coming over again. This time her hands were on her hips and she looked mad, with color coming into her cheeks. She was a blonde and her blue eyes flashed.

'Pa, where're you goin' now?' she demanded.

Ackerman wheeled around, exasperated. Then, acting almost as though she could prevent him from going, he quickly hopped into the saddle where he could have the advantage of being able to stare down at her. Once on the big dun he was a different man, and he pranced and wheeled and guided the horse with his knees and reins. He was an

37

excellent horseman.

'I'm takin' a ride with Talkative, that's where I'm goin'. He needs a talker an' I aim to be it. You can see for yourself the "talker" he carries on his hip; you ain't seen many guns like it, but I have. Look how the end of the barrel sticks out of the holster, and there ain't no front sight. I'll tell you somethin', Sally. Purple Valley has herself a gunfighter; that sight is filed away so that the gun will jump out of the leather like a rattler's tongue. Now you get in the house while I take our neighbor across the valley and help him to get his hoss back. I kinda like Talkative Walker and I don't want to see him jump out that gun, and in two seconds spoil everything he's built up in the last two years of livin' alone in the brakes. Get some lunch goin' for when we get back with the damn jinx hoss!'

'You be careful, you old windbag. It's not him I'm worrying about, it's you. I'm afraid you'll talk yourself to death or wear out your voice. Put your tongue back in its holster and get out of here. Get your own lunch,' she shouted.

'Sure you don't want to borrow one of my horses?' asked Ackerman as they moved out of the yard, scattering the wandering chickens.

'No, this mule is a fast walker,' Jim answered, glancing up at the sun. He was afraid they had lost valuable time.

'She's a nice gal, Sally is, but her tongue's

pure pizen at times. She'll have a bite ready when we get back.'

Walker knew he wasn't coming back if the theory as to where Dodge had hidden the horse was wrong. He had made up his mind that he would stay on the trail of the animal if it took a week. He glanced down at his Winchester; he could live off the land if he had to, he had done it before. His mouth turned grim; it was too bad they had to steal his horse. He thought about the last man that had stolen a horse from him, and there was no question now in his mind about ownership. This horse was his and whoever took him would pay and pay dear, even if Jim had to leave the Purple Valley and start looking again for a place far from trouble.

CHAPTER FIVE

They came down out of the wooded slopes of pine and pinon where Ackerman's ranch was located and swung out onto the knee-deep, grassy plain of Purple Valley. The valley rolled and swelled gently, the deep grass waving in the morning sun. Ahead of them was the gloomy, semiwooded territory known as Cat Hills where Ackerman was sure that the men of Bart Dodge had taken the horse.

After Ackerman ran dry, talking about

everything in and out of the valley, they finally rode in silence, enjoying the good crisp air and the inspiring scenery with the surrounding mountains for a backdrop.

As they traveled, Walker thought of the past two years. He was an outsider here, after having drifted in and buying the small ranch in the high land near the brakes. He had kept apart from the others and he knew little of what was going on in the valley itself. His contacts with the people were limited to those times when he came to town for his meager supplies. Actually, he had done quite well with the small ranch. He had built up his herd and was making enough on the few cows he sold to break even on the supplies he needed.

He had few friends. Morton, the storekeeper in Purple, had tried to be friendly but Walker had preferred to keep to himself. He suspected that the merchant favored him because he had always paid cash. Walker, by nature, was suspicious of everyone. After a long while, he had had two years of peace. Two years when he was not forced to wear a gun, to face anyone down, to meet a challenge or to prove his own skill and courage.

His had been a lonely life, so lonely that he suddenly glanced with relief and gratitude at Ackerman whose conversation had been as welcome as a thunderstorm after a long drouth. Walker liked to read and for that he was thankful. Still a man needs someone besides himself to talk with, and Jim Walker had been too long without anyone to talk to. He was glad that Silver Cloud's theft at least had given him an excuse to visit the Ackerman ranch. He planned to return as often as they would have him, if he got his horse back and everything turned out all right.

Walker wondered what was waiting for them at the Pitchfork line shack in the hills. A gunfight could mean the end of his stay in the valley. He might be run out, forced to leave because of something he had neither wanted nor expected to happen.

He had tasted the thrill of owning the stallion, the horse he had conquered at risk of his own life. The animal was his by every right, for Dodge had made a foolish promise but he had had ample time to back out of it before Jim had touched a stirrup. The rancher's pride and assurance that Jim would fail had kept him from backing down. Silver Cloud was Jim's and always would be; no bunch of six—or sixty—riders could ever take him away and keep him.

The girl was also welcome to his thoughts. Like the conversation of Ackerman, so pleasing to his ears, the sight of her was a blessing to his eyes, and they were both brought about as a result of Silver Cloud coming to him. He felt that the horse was good luck to him and he

41

couldn't see that the horse had been a jinx, so far as he was concerned. Perhaps the horse just wasn't meant to be owned by the other people.

Ackerman reached across and snapped him out of his reverie by pulling on his shirt sleeve. Jim blinked his eyes and followed the old man's pointing finger down the long slope below the crest they were perched on.

The land fell away to a small creek and then rose again on the other side. In the crease near the creek stood a small shack. In a corral nearby, two horses grazed quietly. One was Silver Cloud. Even at that distance, his coat was a mass of silver shining in the noonday sun.

A trace of smoke rose from the slanting tin stack on the shack's roof; other than that there was no sign of life. They started down slowly, picking the easy way but always keeping the door of the shack in plain sight. As they drew near, the stallion put his head into the air and trumpeted a salute, for he had caught their scent and was now standing warily, a little apart from the other horse. Ackerman's zebra dun whickered shrilly as they came within a few hundred yards of the cabin and the silver stallion gave a shrill return answer.

There was a crash inside the board shack as though someone had dropped a pan, and a man shouldered his way into the doorway.

'Neal Spaker,' grunted Ackerman, from the side of his mouth. 'One of Dodge's boys. You won't be able to push him far. He don't bend.'

Walker grunted and reached down to ease the loop off the hammer of his Colt. They walked the mule and the horse in slow and easy, never taking their eyes off the cowboy. He in turn focused on them carefully and didn't move from the doorway. Walker noted that he was a southpaw and that he leaned easily against the door jamb with his right shoulder; his left hand—his gun hand—was loosely draped against his side with his thumb hooked into his belt. He had but to drop his hand six inches to reach the low-slung iron on his hip.

He was a lean, freckled redhead in his middle thirties, with a steady appraising eye that never wavered or blinked as the two riders came closer. He knew he was caught cold as far as the stallion was concerned, yet he still maintained a confident, unconcerned air.

Walker and Ackerman stopped their mounts not ten yards from the shack.

Spaker spoke first. 'Howdy, gents. Somethin' I can do for yuh?'

Walker stirred in the saddle; he still wanted to live in peace, and he didn't want old Ackerman to stop a bullet because of him.

'I come over here to get my horse,' Walker declared. Spaker smiled. 'Oh! Is he wearin' your brand, pard?'

'I ain't had time to fix the brand, mister. How about goin' back to your lunch while my friend and I rope him out of that corral?' Walker replied.

'This hoss belongs to Mister Dodge. Mister Dodge sez, "Neal, you take this hoss out tuh the Cat Hills an' let him chaw thet blue grass." So I brung the critter out here an' I ain't aboot tuh turn him loose to no ornery mule-rideh!'

'Okay, I'll take him, anyway, bud.' Walker started for the corral on the mule.

'Hold it a mite!' declared Spaker. There was a big Colt in his hand and he waved Walker away from the corral.

Walker stopped the mule.

Ackerman rocked back and forth uneasily in his stirrups. He was still in his original position and out of the line of fire.

'Better not try that kind of stuff, Neal,' he said. 'Walker, here, is in his rights in comin' for that hoss, an' I reckon you know it as well as I. I see you pack o' fools comin' down from Walker's las' night an' I see you takin' the stallion. Now Walker ain't a negative guy, an' if you're expectin' him to plead with you or try to talk this hoss back onto his rope, then you're plumb loco. I sashayed over here with him to see that nobody got hurt, 'cause I knew that if he didn't have nobody to do his talkin' for him, then there'd be trouble. Now here you are, about to let go with a lesson from Teacher Colt.'

'Yuh better make that mule jump backwards, Walker, or yo're gonna slope across this valley afoot. I ain't aboot tuh hang this ole iron on a peg,' Spaker threatened.

Walker sighed, but made no move toward his own gun. He sat with his hands folded over the pommel of the saddle, the reins entwined in his fingers. His eyes never left those of the cowboy.

'You'd best put your six-shooter away like Mister Ackerman advised, old son, or I'll kill you as dead as that stone by your foot,' Walker said softly. Still he made no threatening move.

'You'll shoot me?' asked Spaker, amazed. He even glanced down at his own pistol, wondering if something was wrong with it. He glanced quickly up, smiling.

'That's right.'

'You don't figure that's a chore that'll be a mite hard, eh, pard? You aren't worryin' just a little aboot the drop I'm holdin'?'

'Not a bit,' began Walker. 'You've still got to cock the gun, redhead. Don't move your thumb. Don't move it a quarter of an inch, 'cause if you do, I'm gonna draw.'

Spaker's lips twitched at his mouth corner. He tipped up the muzzle of his gun slightly. Spaker was an excellent shot but he had never heard bragging such as this and he wanted to shoot off the hat of the loud-mouthed Walker. He knew it wasn't possible for Walker to draw, cock and fire in the space of time it would take his own thumb to cock the hammer and let it fall on a shell. There was nothing in his eyes but blank depths, for he knew the signals that could be read in a person's eyes. His thumb began the movement, and he heard his own Colt smash the silence. He saw Walker's hat fly through the air, and then he felt the returning slug of Walker's Colt drive him crashing into the cabin.

It had been a blur of two-handed movement, for lightning seemed to take hold of Jim Walker in that instant before the fire flashed from Jim's Colt. He saw the fear on Walker's face as the .45 slug ripped through his hat, not an inch above his forehead. Too late, Spaker realized that Walker had thought he had shot to kill, and somehow Walker had made the fastest draw Spaker had ever witnessed.

Ackerman and Walker tumbled into the one-room shack and kneeled at Spaker's side. He had crashed into the table and knocked over two chairs. His blue shirt was soaking with the bright red of his lifeblood. A tiny trickle came from the corner of his mouth as he labored for breath. The expression in his eyes was the terrified look of a man dying without family or friends near. Ackerman held up his head.

'I'm cut out o' the bunch,' the Pitchfork cowboy groaned.

'I reckon you are, Spaker. I'm sorry that I was the one that culled you,' apologized Jim.

'That's all right. I was jus' fixin' tuh blow yore hat off, pard. I can see why a feller wouldn't cotton to a joke like that. I see the

46

look in yore eye,' Neal croaked, his voice falling.

'You sure scared me,' admitted Walker.

'Whiskey—there on the shelf,' muttered the cowboy.

Ackerman stepped to the shelf and got the partly filled quart bottle, pulling the cork with his teeth. The old man handed the bottle to the dying puncher.

Spaker held the bottle out, offering them some.

'Don't wanta ask yuh to drink after a dead man,' he grinned weakly. He placed the bottle to his mouth and some went down his throat and some down his chin as he drank his fill. His eyes started to glaze over and suddenly he sprang forward as though awakening from a dream. Seeing the alarmed looks on their faces, he settled back with a chuckle. 'Don't look so damn scared. I'm the one thet's goin' down the trail!' He drank some more and the bottle was empty. He set it down gently almost as if it were important not to break it in this final hour.

Spaker closed his eyes and smiled, murmuring: 'Damn hoss ain't worth dyin' fer, pard. Why don't yuh leave him in the corral—or shoot 'im? He—'

Walker stared at Ackerman. This was probably the end for him in the valley. He still couldn't believe it had happened; if only he hadn't worn his gun, a man would be alive. The fool apparently had tried to shoot off his hat, but how could he have known that? They never believed how fast he was. It had always been like this, for men threw themselves away when they came against his gun. Now the people in the Purple Valley would learn of his deadliness through Ackerman.

They placed a blanket over Spaker and left him, after turning his horse loose. They knew that the animal would head for the Dodge ranch and bring someone back to take care of Spaker. Silver Cloud whinnied excitedly when they roped him and led him out of the corral. Walker walked to the horse and rubbed his nose; the animal didn't seem too wild, but Jim could see the light in the horse's eyes and he knew Silver Cloud had plenty of bucks in him if it came to a ride.

They slanted back across the valley in the direction they had come, taking the silver stallion with them. They met one valley family in their wagon on the way to town. Walker knew the news would soon be out that he had the horse and he wondered if everybody knew already that the beast had been stolen from him during the night. Knowing Dodge and his men, he wouldn't have been surprised if there had been some bragging.

Of course, there was the matter of Spaker still to come up and again Walker was glad that Ackerman had been along to back up his story of what happened. Once more it seemed that the silver stallion was bringing him luck, at least there was a reliable witness to the killing. He was sorry that Spaker was dead, but he kept trying to put the blame on Dodge where he felt it rightly belonged. Dodge had stolen the horse and Dodge had given Neal his orders.

As they moved swiftly, the mule in a fast walk and the two horses in a half-trot, he found his stomach was knotted with the old feeling. He was sick to death of killing and the worry of when it would stop, or could stop, kneaded his soul.

He glanced at the Purple range, with its lofty, snow-covered peaks, and only the thought that they were eternal while he was here but for a short time saved him from breaking down. He knew he had to keep trying. There must be somewhere he could live without having to kill; perhaps he could stay here. There was Sally Ackerman. Perhaps the horse would bring him good luck, for he had never owned a horse that was half the animal Silver Cloud was.

CHAPTER SIX

The rest of the trip across the valley passed without their seeing another soul. Before long they were turning the animals into the corral at

Ackerman's, Walker having agreed to stay for supper. The sun was dropping behind the Purples, leaving a red and blue sky that would not be light for long. Before they turned from the chore of feeding and graining the animals, a dull glow of lamplight was coming from the glass squares of the cabin's windows.

Ackerman had installed a pump and going to this they took turns pumping for each other and washing in the ice-cold water. A pump was a wonderful thing, Walker decided, and he resolved to get one the following spring. It was a lot less troublesome to work the pump handle and make the water spew forth than cranking up a bucket on the end of a windlass.

They went inside and, while Sally Ackerman didn't even nod at him, he noted that she had changed her dress. She wore a gingham dress that fell halfway between her ankles and knees, and the neckline was cut square and low. The sight of such daring made Walker search the rough walls for something less stirring at which to stare. The room was swimming in the scent of English lavender, and the loner glanced quickly at the girl and then away again.

In the morning when they had left for the Cat Hills, Sally's hair had been hanging to her shoulders, combed straight and tied back with a bit of red ribbon; but this evening her hair had been somehow transformed into soft, glowing blonde curls that clustered at the back of her head. When she flounced them they caught the light of the lamp and hearth and fairly took away Walker's breath. Her smooth tanned skin was radiant and lovely.

Old Ackerman crashed about the place, getting the things he wanted, paying no heed to the guest who stood in the middle of the room, hat in hand. Jim was obviously embarrassed as to where he should settle his bulk in the small room so bustling with the activities of Ackerman and young Sally.

'Over here! Sit over here, Walker. By Gawd, I've got the medicine in this jug that will cut the fog in your throat. Lasso a chair and drop down here at the table with me. Now, how about four fingers' worth?' He raised a clear glass demijohn that when full must have held four or five gallons. Now it was only half full of amber liquid; he poured into one of two tin cups and the contents sloshed to the brim.

The handling of the jug was a two-handed effort for old Ackerman, as the container stood nearly two feet in height and was slightly over a foot in diameter.

'Just give me a part of a cup,' murmured Jim.

Sally came to the table and set down a stack of dishes and condiments for the coming meal not far from Walker's place. He shifted uneasily under her steady, cool gaze as she pulled up a chair.

'Well, you two look pale as ghosts,' she said.

'I see that you got the horse back, and I'd think that you'd be happy and pleased.'

'I'm glad I got the horse back,' mumbled Jim.

'But he ain't glad he had to whisk out his Colt and smash a feller's wishbone to turn the trick,' Ackerman cackled, drinking down the remainder of what was in his cup.

'Oh, no!' exclaimed Sally.

'Yep,' said Ackerman. 'Neal Spaker is as cold as this here whiskey jug. Come mornin', they'll be throwin' dirt in his face over to Dodge's buryin' plot.'

'How awful,' moaned the girl, but she made no effort to leave the table.

Walker shifted his feet where they were stretched out before him, and stared at his battered boots. He could feel her burning glance fall on his face. He wanted to jump up to go, but instead he drank more of the whiskey.

'You don't like it, do you?' He heard the question and felt her hand on his forearm where his sleeve was rolled back a few turns. Her palm felt so smooth and creamy that the touch shocked Walker. He glanced up and his eyes locked with hers. For a moment they stared and he found in her gaze something strange. It was sympathy and understanding, and he was not used to it.

'It's not something you forget as quickly as that,' he said, snapping his fingers. 'It's not like

52

swatting a fly or a mosquito. When you kill a man there are lots of things to torment you.'

'Bah, there ain't not!' jeered old Ackerman. 'Besides, Spaker pulled his gun and shot Jim's hat off before the lad here even went for his Colt. Jim warned Neal; he says, "You still gotta cock your gun, redhead, an' that's time enough for me to pull!" That's what he says, so help me!'

'Is that how it was?' asked the girl.

Jim nodded.

'How do you know what it's like to kill, you old windbag,' yelled the girl, turning on old Ackerman. 'Who'd you ever kill?'

Ackerman shook his head and blinked his eye. He was seldom at a loss for words, and he came back:

'Why, who'd I ever shoot, you says? Didn't I tell you fifty times about the time I was in the posse that got Harry Brown? It was in seventy-two an' your maw, she begged me not to go when the posse was stampin' their hosses aroun' in the dust. But I grabbed my old Rem rollin' block—it's still a-hangin' there on the pegs by the fire-place. See her, Walker? Well, we caught Harry at the sand banks—you know where that is.

'We knew he was in there somewhere, 'cause his hoss was left lame at the beginnin' of the sand banks. We went sneakin' in after him. They was twenty of us, mostly boys from the saloon in Purple. They wasn't good shots neither, an' we was all liquored a bit and scared as hell. I reckon Harry Brown was the calmest man in the sand banks that night. You see, we found out the next day that Harry was innocent. Shucks, he never shot Ned Bray at all, it was some saddle tramp that done it.

'Anyway, Harry lured us through the sand banks like a smart ole cat and when we was halfway in on foot, he somehow got aroun' behind us and made a dash for our hosses that we'd left with only Jack Archer, the town halfwit, to guard 'em. But we all spun aroun' and started to cut loose at Brown. Now that was where the lyin' of that night begun. I swear he streaked across my sights jus' as I squeezed off. There must have been twenty out o' twenty that cut loose with lead and we kept on firin' 'cause Harry was no slouch with a gun. He went down in the first burst but we give him a couple o' more volleys to make sure he wasn't bluffin'. We kilt a couple o' our hosses, too, as I recollect. Also Jack Archer, o' course, who was in the line of fire. I always said I was the one who really got him, but a dozen others took the credit. Of course, no one would vouch as to who killed young Archer. It was Brown's fault, anyhow.'

'Pay no attention to him,' said the girl, 'every night he has one cup of whiskey before dinner and that's all he can take. From now on he'll

54

just be raving and you and I can talk.'

'Maybe I ought to go?' queried Walker.

'Certainly not, not after what you've been through. Why don't you tell me more about it; perhaps it would unburden you to talk. What are some of the things that you say will torment you? It *was* self defense.'

'In spite of that,' Walker began, 'there's a terrible feeling of guilt. You look down at the dying man and you say, "Thou shalt not kill." You don't think it out loud, but it's in your mind. And when you kill it's ringing in your ears like a church bell. You tell yourself that it's self-defense, but even if the man is a murderer, people will still walk around you in the street like you were a menace. A killer is never liked; he's respected, maybe, but never liked or accepted by folks as a friend or a neighbor.'

'That's not true. I know little about you and yet I find myself liking you more and more,' replied the girl.

He did not answer directly, but continued on the same line:

'Then you have to fear revenge. No matter how brave you are, it's a menace because those who are vengeful justify any kind of a sneak attack. Every time you kill a fellow, no matter how fair the fight, you have to figure that he probably has relatives who'll come looking for your hide, and they'll take it any way they can get it. Then you have to fear the law—a man's survivors can make the law take more turns than a snake. The worst outlaw, when killed, can turn into a saint in the eyes of the law, and some folks believe that a killing must be legally punished. Then, there are the ghosts that come at night.'

'Ghosts?' said the girl.

'I don't mean the kind you imagine you see. I mean the men you've killed that keep appearing in your dreams. Some nights it's better not to lie down at all because they parade before your eyes constantly, always threatening you with vengeance. So you see, you're never really rid of the man you kill.'

Walker could see the compassion and understanding in the girl's eyes, and the look amazed him.

'You sit and have another drink if you want. I'll put on supper now,' she said.

Sally rushed to a hissing kettle and rescued the contents, pouring it into a bowl. From the solid black stove she took a large, heavy roast from the oven and two steaming pies from another section. These she set on the stone mantel to cool. There were potatoes, and greens from the garden. The delicious rare roast beef, the girl sliced into slabs a half-inch thick and piled onto Jim's plate. She had freshly baked bread and sweet butter and small cakes made with a corn batter. A huge pot of coffee was brought from the fire and set on the table.

Walker went to work on the food. Old Ackerman became strangely silent, his tongue somehow immobilized by the management of the food and the effect of the whiskey. Jim's mind roved; how long had it been since he had tasted cooking like this with the delicately added spice and flavoring. His cooking had been that of the loner and the trail camp, with the essentials provided because a man must eat to work but he didn't need to have the woman's touch to survive. He piled the sweet, fresh-churned butter on the soft, warm bread and swabbed it through the rich red roast-beef gravy, and cleared his plate so that it appeared completely clean. It had been his second heaping plateful and he sat back and patted his stomach. Sally set a wedge of pie before him and poured more of the steaming coffee. She sat on the edge of her chair with her chin resting on her hand, her elbow propped on the table. She regarded him happily and when he asked for a second quarter of the pie she was delighted beyond words.

Old Ackerman belched, excused himself, and headed for the door. As he went his pipe was digging into his tobacco pouch. They heard him sit down on the bench outside the door where he customarily had his smoke while Sally was doing the dishes.

Walker built a cigarette as the girl was clearing the wreckage of the meal. He snapped a match alive with his thumbnail and sucked the flame against the flimsy cigarette. He puffed slowly and blew the smoke from his mouth and nose. He knew he should be starting for the ranch and yet he hated to go. He stood up and began helping her with the dishes.

'Oh, you don't have to,' she murmured.

'I don't mind. I do them all the time up at the shack.'

'Why do you call it a shack?' she asked, obviously not liking the word.

'Well, that's about all it is,' he replied.

'It's almost as good as this place,' she declared.

'Someday I'd like to have a nice house up there,' he confided.

'It's so beautiful up there,' Sally said. 'I used to ride that way often when nobody was there—the air's so clear and the smell of the pine is like heaven.'

Walker smiled blankly; it was plain that he was envisioning the place in his own mind. Hard against the mountains, the ranch had no neighbors to the north, the lonely brakes were to the west. Sparkling water dashed and danced in a twisting, rushing brook down from the eternal snow-caps of the Purples. To the east the rolling tiers of hills were all his, and his cattle grazed in grass up to their bellies, grass that was forever green and watered by the seepage from the snow-water streams of the

Purples. A man could never run a large number of cattle on the land he owned, even two thousand head would be too many. But a man could live nicely on what he had, once a good herd was built up. And a woman could live with him because there was enough for two, and more left over for a family. If a man wanted something for his sons to hang onto and make wealth from, there were the tall trees that ranged the Purples clear to the timber line. Straight virgin stands of choice wood in amounts that would stagger the imagination, forests so thick and high that the sunlight hadn't reached the pine-needle floor in a hundred years. There was no need for timber in the Purple Valley now, but someday more people would come and Walker would have the timber. It was a long way off and still if Sally should become his wife, then their children might realize such a dream.

Jim snapped out of his reverie.

'You should come up there more often. Now that we know each other, I could show you around the place,' Jim offered.

'That'd be nice,' she smiled. 'Say, do you dance?'

Jim's heart leaped for he thought surely that she was going to suggest that they dance together now. He glanced around the room, relieved to see no phonograph.

'Well, I'm not too good at it, but I like it,' he

59

admitted.

'Good.' She smiled, turning to him. 'There's a dance in Purple next Saturday night. Why don't we go together?'

'Why, that'd really be something,' Walker said, pleased.

The dishes were done and he found himself awkwardly trying to say something besides goodbye but the words wouldn't come to him and he slipped out the door and went to the corral. Old Ackerman, tired by the long ride, was snoring on the bench by the cabin door and Jim decided not to awaken him. He saddled the mule and brought the stallion along on the lead rope. He smiled all the way to the shack and when he got there he found that the mustang had wandered in for some grain.

He raised the corral bars and stood in the moonlight a long time, watching the stallion and wondering if such a great horse was indeed the turning point of his fortunes.

CHAPTER SEVEN

The week dragged for Walker because he spent long restless nights getting out of bed at all hours and looking out the window to check on the silver stallion in the corral. He rigged up some crude warning devices in case someone should come sneaking around in the dark. During the day he worked on the stallion, getting his confidence, grooming him, giving him all sorts of kindness but nevertheless going through a painful period of saddle and bridle training before each day was over.

On Monday Silver Cloud trembled all over from shoulder to fetlock upon viewing the saddle intended for him. On Tuesday he merely shied away from it. On Wednesday he accepted the encumbrance with scarcely a show of annoyance. By Thursday he realized that the rewards of sweet things and tasty grain were worth the trouble. A half-dozen leaps were all the bucks he gave on that day and Walker took him out of the corral and rode him rapidly down the softly carpeted pine-needle trail of the forest. They shot out of the trees and into the rolling tier of hills that comprised the eastern section of Jim's land.

At a smooth gallop they swept around his small herd of contented cattle. The beeves, knee-deep in the lush pasture of the upper lands, paused and looked up at the horse and rider flashing by, then went back to munching the grass.

As they pelted along, Walker was more delighted than he had ever been in his life, with the great ribs of Silver Cloud sprung outward between his legs, with the smooth-flowing stride of the great horse bearing him along, the wind roaring in his face and the silver mane of the horse flying back and mingling with his fingers on the reins. Running power and lasting strength such as this he had never felt but he was feeling it now. 'Heart' they called it and a judge would note it by the great chest of the horse. But Jim was feeling it first-hand—the only real way—by running the horse hard and long.

Silver Cloud fell to the task with a will and let some of his frustration loose by reaching forward with his legs on each bound and eating up the rolling ground they rode over. The horse seemed happy running like this and not so much of the sullen, beaten captive he had appeared for most of the week. Walker resolved to give the horse such a ride often. For, with all the running he had already done, he scarcely labored for breath. There was a fine coating of sweat on his body but it wasn't the sweat of hard labor. Walker loosed the reins and let the animal have his head. Silver Cloud stretched his chin and aimed for the horizon. Now he found more stride than he had before and his ride became a flowing progression of muscular power with no shock of striking hoofs thrown back to the rider. Instead, it was just the steady undulating sway of an easy gallop and Walker swore that the horse could run no faster.

Before Walker realized what had happened they were down out of the upper hills and into the smoother floor of the valley. Jim drew up in surprise as he topped the rise of ground that shielded the main trail from Purple. Below him on the heavily rutted road a group of horsemen also fought their horses to a standstill. Jim cursed because of all the people he could have blundered upon he had to pick a group of Pitchfork riders, led by Lash Wade.

They appeared to be coming from town and with eager cries they all pointed to the quarry; out of the jumble of wheeling and plunging horses came Wade's mount, leaping forth to take the lead after being spurred and quirted by the Pitchfork foreman. Walker knew that now the fighting men Dodge hired would be after him for more than just the horse; they would be riding to exact payment for the death of Neal Spaker.

To ride back through his own lonely lands might have seemed the safest course, but Walker didn't deem it so. Few people rode that far into the hills except rarely, when chasing strays or hunting. His best bet would be to escape directly into the valley where, at least if he were overtaken, he would be closer to witnesses in front of whom the Pitchfork riders might hesitate to kill him. He reined the stallion to the side and plunged down the slope at an angle aimed at hitting the valley road ahead of the Pitchfork crew.

There was a shout from the pursuers as they

descried his attempted course and soon the stallion brought him onto the road a hundred yards ahead of the others.

Now he cursed his foolishness in riding the stallion so hard all the way from the ranch. The Pitchfork horses were probably fresh; certainly they had not been running when he had the bad luck to blunder into them. He plunged ahead. Looking back, he could see that his pursuers seemed to be coming along easily, content to hold him in sight and run the stallion to death. Then another thought came to him—every step along this road was another step closer to Bart Dodge's Pitchfork headquarters. Ahead he saw a rutted trail branching off to the left through the trees. This was the road to the Weavers—a small family spread not too active in valley affairs. Jim swung off the trail and followed the narrow ruts through the grass.

When Walker looked back, after following the Weaver road for a few minutes, the riders behind him were grouped about as before, with Lash Wade coming on rapidly, although the fantastic running power of Silver Cloud had widened the gap to a half-mile.

Beyond the second hummock, he came in to a stretch of country little known to himself but excellently suited to his role in this deadly game of hide-and-seek. Before him ranged a whole series of hills of the drumlin variety and in those vast, tumbling land-waves, left thousands of years ago by the glaciers, he could spur his horse over any one of them before the Pitchfork riders topped the rise behind him. Then they would have to guess where he had gone.

He headed for a hill on his left. Careful inspection of the grass would reveal his trail, but if they took time for that, he could confuse them on the next hill, and in this way he could lengthen the distance between them. He seemed safe, and once over the first hill he chose the next and headed for it, drawing up on the far side and watching the horse labor for breath. He jumped off and quickly tightened the cinches, then whirled the reins around the horse's forefeet in a tight hobble and raced back to the crest of the hill. He crawled on all fours the last few feet and parted the tall grasses to peer forth. His heart was gladdened by the sight of them riding to his right in a little depression and, with each step of their tired horses, passing farther away. They were at least a mile off.

Jim ran back to the stallion. Grasping the stirrup, he mounted and headed the horse around to the left of the hill. He went at a steady lope, not daring to walk the horse too much for fear that the Pitchfork men would realize their mistake and press after him, shrinking the gap before he knew it.

He believed his best chance was to get back to the ranch by the route he had come, for with all the shooting, men from other parts of the valley might come riding to investigate—including other riders from Pitchfork.

To get his bearings, he headed again for the valley road. Sighting it at last, he brought the inexhaustible stallion to a lope and made for the open country. Then an anguished cry of dismay came from him as he sighted another group of riders.

This time there was no mistaking their intention. They gave shout and spur the moment they sighted him. Jim, taking a quick glance over his shoulder, recognized Bart Dodge himself in the lead of his gun-hung riders. Jim cursed and swung back into the drumlins at a gallop, his one idea to run as level a course as possible to outdistance this new bunch of Pitchfork punchers.

Turning and twisting in the drumlins, he lost them and glanced up to the sun for direction, pausing to listen for sounds of pursuit. To his left and behind him he could hear the steadily fading jingle of their harness and the pelting of hoofs diminish in the distance. Sighing in relief, he realized now that he could swing west and follow the valley road as far as the Ackerman place, where Dodge would be reluctant to take violent action against him before such witnesses as Dan Ackerman and his daughter.

A sudden shout went up behind him and glancing around he was amazed to see Lash

66

Wade at the head of his group of horsemen coming down the side of a hill. Apparently they had picked up fresh horses at the Weaver ranch because Jim recognized none of the mounts as those that had been following him before. As if to signal the end, Silver Cloud stumbled and made Jim's heart thump but the horse recovered and they shot ahead once more, with the stallion still reaching magnificently. But the extra stride was gone now and the pace he set barely held even with that of the fresh ponies behind him.

Walker's legs were drenched with the sweat from Cloud's sides. Foam was flying from the horse's mouth, yet he didn't need the quirt. Cloud labored now with his great heart beating out against his ribs and Walker could feel the beating against his thighs. This made him furious. He wanted to turn and ride back at them with his gun blazing death for each one. For himself he cared nothing, had been living too long on borrowed time already, but for the horse a reckless charge could mean death.

One thing was sure, Jim told himself. He would keep on as long as he thought the horse would not be ruined, but he would not ride beyond that point. He would surrender the horse and take his own stand in some sheltered spot. Sufficient rage was building in him to kill, but now that he was ready for them, he found that he respected them for not shooting at the horse, which they would have done on any other occasion.

He didn't know if he could make it to Ackerman's place or not, and suddenly he realized what a stronghold the valley was for Dodge. Here the rancher was riding around in broad daylight with a dozen armed men, trying to kill him and steal his horse. How, Walker asked himself, could he continue to live in such a place as this? Another shout behind him cut short his musing and he knew they were gaining with the fresh horses. A long, hard slope lay ahead and he tried to help the stallion by shifting his weight forward in the stirrups. As they made the top, the lower part of the valley spread out before him once more; to his right the road swung wide into the flat, fertile land. Across his path lay the cutoff to Ackerman's and the pine woods beyond that. As he headed for the low ranch house, a group of horsemen broke out of the trees on his right where the hill became wooded. Jim was amazed to see that Dodge had anticipated his movement and had ridden at breakneck speed through the drumlins. Clearly, Dodge now aimed to intercept him as he got to the Ackerman spread.

Behind Jim, Lash Wade and his five riders were coming hard, while below him and to his right spurred Dodge's bunch, his men shouting for the kill. Jim was so high that they all looked like toys as they came out of the distance. He could see a blur of movement at the Ackerman ranch, where he was apparently doomed to arrive in a tie with Dodge. To rein back and go the other way was impossible; Silver Cloud was dangerously low, his running reserve gone, but he stumbled on, going on heart alone.

Now came an even more perplexing event. Out of the pines above Ackerman's place, near the spot where the trail led up to his own ranch, swept a third group of horsemen. They started fanning out to prevent Jim from arriving at the Ackerman place. His heart sank and he drew rein, watching the riders come on behind him and to the side as well as from the front. They hemmed him in and as he watched them come closer, he realized that he must be quite a sight. His clothes were sweat-soaked and caked with dust. He pulled off his hat and angrily wiped the band, sweat streaming from his brow. It had been a hard ride, but a failure nevertheless, for Dodge had won. Nothing now could stop him from taking the horse. But the important question was, how much more would he take?

CHAPTER EIGHT

Walker was concerned by the presence of Sheriff Wally Bristol from the town of Purple. At first he had not recognized the lawman as the leader of the group of horsemen that had come from the pines above Ackerman's place. Bristol was in his fifties, a small, lean man, tanned and whitehaired. He had a seamed, weather-beaten face. Walker knew that the presence of Bristol had something to do with the shooting of Spaker.

As always, when large mounted groups come together facing one another, there is difficulty in calming the horses and one rider or another has trouble with his mount. To add to the shouting and hollering of the cowboys as they manipulated their mounts, there was the stamping of hoofs and the jingle and rattle of harness; besides all this the dust they had kicked up came rolling with the wind, leaving the men coughing and cursing.

Jim Walker warily watched the tightening circle, his hands on the saddle horn. While Bristol was calling for silence and choking on the dust, Jim glanced at the men that surrounded the lawman. Those accompanying the sheriff were all townsmen; they sat their horses indifferently, waiting to hear what the sheriff was going to say.

The rest of the men were all Pitchfork riders, and in the pay of Bart Dodge. They sat looking at him with eager expectancy, their pistols drawn and cocked. The chase had been a hard one and now that the quarry was run down, they were eager for the next move. Dodge himself had not as yet drawn a gun and he sat his saddle wiping the dust and grime from his face with a fine linen handkerchief. Walker felt as he always did when in Dodge's presence; he kept trying to recall where he had seen the man before, outside of this stretch of country.

Dodge had black wavy hair and a small mustache, fastidiously trimmed, that he was constantly stroking with thumb and forefinger. His face was full, with a high, wide forehead and his dark-brown eyes were set far apart. He was handsome and usually pleasant-appearing, and was popular in town and on the range.

At the moment, Dodge was wearing a tight-lipped smile of victory and sight of the smug expression infuriated Walker. What the devil was so familiar-appearing about the man? Where, Walker wondered for the hundredth time, could he have seen him before?

The dust finally stopped billowing, the horses whickered or shifted their feet as they quieted down. Saddles creaked and groaned as the men moved their weight. They were tense and ready for Dodge's next orders.

Walker held the stallion with firm knees and a steady hand on the reins to avoid any sudden movement, for he could see the pistols at full cock, all trained on him.

Sheriff Bristol turned to Walker. 'Well, you got that critter, so you can ride him, eh?' he said admiringly.

'Never mind that; let's get a rope around his scrawny neck,' Lash Wade grumbled.

'Hold your mouth, Lash,' Bristol broke in.

'Why? He's a killer and a horse thief,' Lash yelled.

'That's a lie,' Walker said flatly, turning and looking Wade in the eye.

'You both can shut up; I'm goin' to do the talkin',' Wally Bristol ordered.

'Wally,' Bart Dodge advised, 'you're making a mistake if you try to take him back for trial. Folks just won't stand hitched for it, and there'll be a lynchin' sure as shooting.'

'You just tell yore boys to drop those sixguns into leather, Bart. I don't like all the artillery wavin' in the air like that.'

Wally Bristol was as calm as a lily pond and his own Colt was buckled inside an old army-issue holster. He stared at the riders with cold, unblinking eyes and some of the gun muzzles tipped downward with his first words.

'The boys want justice,' Dodge said.

'They'll get it. I doubt if they really want it, but if they holster them irons they'll get it and if they don't, they'll maybe get six ounces of forty-four! Now you boys do like I say an' holster those guns, and point them at the ground when you're easin' them off-cock. I don't want none of you to say yore gun went off accidental and just happened to perforate Mister Walker, here. If I should hear any of you claim a thing like that, I'll shoot the son-of-a-gun.'

The men looked sullenly at Dodge. The ranch owner was perturbed by Wally Bristol but he shrugged in resignation and the men carefully put up their guns.

'That's a damned sight nicer lookin',' commented Bristol. 'Now, let's just complete the picture by you fellas movin' yore hosses over there in the background—say about a pistol shot and a half distance, eh?'

Again the men glanced at Dodge and Wade.

'Better tell them to go, Dodge. I'll be big about it an' let Wade sit and listen to the palaver.'

'Okay, boys, do as the sheriff says,' Dodge grumbled.

'Why, that's real nice o' you, Bart. Now, you five fellas with me, you don't want to hear none of this, so you go over there about half a pistol shot distance and just set yore hosses between Captain Dodge and his crew. That'll leave us three to jaw a little!'

The possemen spurred their horses to the spot the sheriff had indicated and Walker drew his first deep breath.

His backbone still tingled from moments before when the guns had been trained on him. A bullet was all he could have expected from the Pitchfork riders who were ready to take revenge for Spaker without regard for any law

73

but the swift, crude justice of the range. Bound by the tight-knit loyalty that comes from riding together in freezing weather and burning drouth, the men who rode for any one brand were a small society unto themselves. Walker had once been one of them and had shared their loyalty and their dangers. So he respected the Pitchfork cowhands because of their craft—not of their brand or their boss.

'You taking this gunfighter's word for things?' queried Dodge. He had composed himself and was twisting a cigarette. There was a trace of a sardonic smile on his lips and his eyes were narrowed and cold, as if to chide the lawman.

Sheriff Wally Bristol spat. 'I ain't ever heard him called gunfighter yet, Bart. I heard him called loner and silent and farmer. I suppose he is a loner if thet's what you call a man who keeps his nose where it belongs. I reckon, too, that you could call him silent because he sure don't run off at the mouth the way some folks do. I suppose that because he grows a few potatoes, you gotta right to call him a farmer. However, I don't see that he's a gunfighter—though he is wearin' a slick-lookin' Colt that I never see before. You a gunfighter, Walker?'

'I didn't pick the fight with Spaker. It was self-defense.'

'That's a lie,' Lash Wade shouted.

'Shut up. It ain't a lie,' scowled Bristol. 'But it was magic the way I heard the story from old Ackerman—that story, by the way, Dodge, was considerable different from the way you told it in town. The way old Ackerman saw the fight, Walker, here, let Spaker have a hundred-yard start and still beat him cold. Anyhow, the whole thing was a mistake, Dodge. Your man thought to be funny and blow the silent loner's hat off. Walker gave Spaker a good warnin', tellin' him not to cock the gun or he'd kill him. How'd you like to sit there and let me blow a few holes through yore Stetson, Lash? Is that the kinda thing you can take without blinkin' an eye?'

'We don't believe that story,' began Dodge. 'No man could—'

'Take a shot at his hat an' see,' laughed Bristol, his eyes twinkling. 'Reckon that's the only way we're gonna find out.'

Lash and Bart looked at one another. They didn't like the way the sheriff was talking and they didn't say anything but a lot passed in their glances. Walker stirred uneasily, wondering what was coming.

Bristol added, 'As for me, I ain't gonna move toward this old hog-leg o' mine—not this afternoon. Now, supposin' he just gets sick of this palaver. Remember, he beat Neal when Neal had his gun drawn, and we all know Neal was fast. It seems to me that he might hit the three of us before we got a shot off. Any o' you

75

see it that way? By golly, maybe Walker, here—that we been callin' loner and silent and farmer all these years—is a better man than any of us. Maybe he *is* a gunfighter, but me, I don't aim to find out!'

Wade's face turned red.

'You just gonna let him go?' he asked. Lash was a fair foreman but he was a slow thinker and it was just beyond his ken that a man like Walker could ever get the best of Dodge.

'Why, what the hell can I hold him on? I oughta run you boys in for hoss-stealin', that's what I oughta do. Now I want all this damn foolishness over that hoss stopped and stopped today, you hear? Just look at the way Walker is riding this hoss, usin' a hackamore for a bridle. A hackamore, mind you. He's treating this mean nag like it was an old toothless plow hoss. And what's more, boys, you had that hoss for three years and there wasn't a man of you that could stay in the saddle when you tried. Now I can see that this is botherin' you, 'cause you know the whole damn valley's laughin' their heads off at those tough Pitchfork galoots.'

'Now wait a minute, Wally,' Dodge said. 'We softened this horse up over the years, and Walker happened to be only there at the right moment.'

'You'd be smart if you let us hang him,' shouted Lash. 'You're headin' for trouble, Bristol. Walker is a gunfighter and an

76

outlaw—he's one of the Wild Bunch.'

Bristol's eyes narrowed. He stared at Walker for a moment as if searching his memory, then he glanced back to Wade.

Walker felt the sweat break out on his neck as old memories came back to haunt him.

'Where'd you boys hear he was one o' the Wild Bunch?' asked Wally slyly.

Lash gazed at Dodge in confusion and waited for the rancher to answer the question.

'Just a rumor, Wally; probably no truth in it. Still I bet if he heard a train whistle he'd pull his bandanna clear up to his eyes.'

The handsome Dodge burst out laughing and the possemen who were straining to hear the conversation also began to guffaw at the remark. It was quickly passed from them to the Pitchfork riders who started to howl over it. Even Bristol had to chuckle and only Walker sat with his face immobile and unsmiling, the setting sun glinting on his high cheekbones.

Bristol wagged his head. 'The things you don't hear when folks get mad at each other. Walker's been livin' up there near the brakes fer nigh onto two years and you never see yore civic duty till just this minute, eh?'

'He's an outlaw, take it from me,' persisted Lash. 'Run him out of the country an' save yoreself a heap of trouble. He's already killed one fella an' he ain't through yet—you wait and see!'

'Okay, Lash, I reckon I kin wait. But if anybody's gonna chase his heels out o' this country I'll do it, and if you or any o' yore riders interfere, I'll run the whole damn lot of you clear across the Purple Mountains. Up to now I been takin' a light view of what's been happenin' over this here damned gift hoss. But a man has been killed, and beginnin' right here I'm gonna try to settle this thing. Dodge, how much will you give for this hoss?'

'The horse ain't for sale,' Walker declared.

Bristol turned. 'I ain't talkin' to you, Walker!'

'I'll give him two hundred dollars but the fool has already said he won't sell for any price,' Dodge growled.

'I don't blame him,' declared Bristol. 'Now you look at the way that hoss is standin'. Then look around at the rest of these nags and see how they's still wheezin' like a pack of whales. Look at how that hoss is standin' with his head up and his ears pricked forward. Where'd you first see this hoss, Lash?'

'Why, we seen him come out of the hills above the Weaver place. He run into us accidental, it seemed.'

'An' I suppose this is still the same hoss that I heard you fellas firing at over in the drumlins, eh?' smiled Bristol.

'Well, for Gawd's sake, o' course this is the same hoss. He sure didn't change hosses on us,' scowled Wade.

'An' I suppose he ran all the way from the drumlins to here with the pack o' you hard after him, eh? Rode for his life, you might say, eh?'

'Of course he did, but I don't see—'

'How far'd this hoss run before you ever saw Wade, Jim?' queried Wally.

'Three, four miles, maybe five. From my ranch to the valley road by way of the hills,' stated Walker flatly.

'There, you hear that, Dodge? An' you offer him two hundred. Why, the sweat on this hoss alone is worth two hundred. Now you know how far this hoss ran an' he still woulda lost the pack of you if I hadn't happened out of the woods into his path. I like to think that Walker stopped out of consideration for the hoss. This is a fifteen-hundred-dollar hoss, an' maybe a smart fella would go as high as two thousand for him—it would depend on what some men thought their life was worth. Now I ain't gonna say that you oughta pay Walker fifteen hundred for this hoss or—'

'Well, of course I know you're not—' broke in Dodge, smiling.

'No, I'm gonna set a thousand dollars as the amount,' interrupted Wally Bristol. 'Because if I owned the horse I wouldn't let go of him fer less.'

'Why, that's ridiculous,' began Dodge. 'I don't have that much money, but if Walker would take seven fifty—'

Bristol burst out laughing. 'By jings, that's about what I'd been hopin' you'd counter with.' He turned to Jim. 'Now, son, you gotta admit that you didn't exactly come by this hoss by normal means. I got you a deal you can be proud of and you can pick yourself up a couple of good nags with the dough. You can't expect Dodge to do more, things being the way they are.'

Wally sat back in the saddle, clearly pleased with his diplomatic triumph.

'Can I get on up to my ranch now?' asked Walker.

The smile faded from Bristol's face. He said, 'Well, if you two ain't the stubbornest steers I ever recollect. All right, I tried my best but it didn't do no good. I bent over backward and kissed my spurs tryin' to straighten this stupid mess out. Walker, I got you a good offer for the hoss. Dodge, I told you what the hoss was worth and you made this bet. Now I'm tellin' you two that if another shot is fired in this valley over this damn hoss, I'll run the one that fires it clear down to the Border!'

Walker reined the stallion around the fiery-tempered sheriff and started for his own place. Bristol sat watching and mumbling to himself as the Pitchfork group pelted away toward their own spread. The sheriff gathered up his men and headed back toward Purple, after making sure that the two parties were separated by a good safe distance.

CHAPTER NINE

Jim found that the long ride and the hard chase had done a lot to increase the bond between himself and the stallion. His emergence from the cabin on Friday morning brought a loud, friendly whicker of recognition from the horse. He went instantly to the animal with lumps of sugar and held them against Silver Cloud's muzzle. The horse quickly licked up the sweet, and nuzzled Walker for more.

As he had for the better part of the week, he spent most of his time babying and training the stallion. The animal apparently had been saddled many times during his long stay at the Pitchfork but his training had stopped at that point, until this man with the lonely, sad-looking eyes had come along.

Sally Ackerman rode up to discuss the dance on Saturday night. As she rode up on her flashy brown and white pinto she found Jim standing in the corral with his arm around the stallion's neck. She swept into the yard and stepped out of the stirrup. She wore a divided riding skirt made of doeskin and a checkered flannel shirt. Her concho-decorated vest was of the same material as the skirt. Her hair was done in two long braided pigtails. As usual, her face was rosy-cheeked and radiant, her eyes sparkling.

Leaving the pinto standing with the reins hitched in the dust, she quickly climbed the corral bars and perched herself on the top. 'You holdin' him up or is he holdin' you up?' she laughed.

'A little of both,' smiled Walker. He patted the stallion's coat and twisted his hand into the rich, silvery strands of mane. The horse twisted his head and whickered.

'Gee, you've sure got him tamed,' she said admiringly.

'Oh, he's not tame, so don't come in here. See the look in his eyes that says he don't have too much faith in humans yet. Me, he likes, but humans, well—'

'I think you're very human!' exclaimed the girl.

'Well, everybody seems to think I should give up this horse. They seem to think that I'm being a stubborn fool to hold Bart Dodge to his word when he said he'd give the horse to me if I could ride him. Maybe I am loco.' He stared back at the horse, ignoring her for a moment.

'Certainly not. I can see how you feel. This horse never was any good to Bart Dodge; he never held the saddle on him long enough to dot an i. I don't think you should give back the horse. And anyhow a lot of people in the Purple

Valley don't like Bart because he rides such a tight cinch on everyone. He ain't a bad guy and he's a little sweet on me. You gotta admit he's a good-lookin' fella.'

Walker looked back at her. 'I don't think he's so good-lookin'.'

'You don't?' she smiled.

'Well, no—I'd say he wasn't good-lookin'.'

'Why? Why'd you say that, Jim?'

Walker started. This was the first time she had used his name, and he liked the sound of her saying it.

'Well—oh, I don't know. I guess I just don't like him, so I don't see how you can like him.'

'He never gave me a horse, so you should like him more than me,' she teased.

'Maybe that's why I don't like him,' laughed Jim. 'Anyway, there's something about that fellow that I remember from somewhere else. How long's he been here in the valley?'

'Oh, five years, I guess; maybe more. Anyway, when he came here he bought in big and got all the Almstock land just when the old man passed on. He paid a big price for the place and folks around here thought he was rich. He started a good-sized herd and marketed some steers the first year. Dad says his water is dryin' up. Just tough luck, I guess. His springs started to go dry about the time he got the stallion, here. He's only got water in two places—in the Cat Hills and near the ranch house. All his cattle are drawn in pretty close to the old house now, with water so short. It looks funny when you ride over there.'

'You go over there often, eh?' There was a touch of sharpness in Walker's voice.

'Sure, I ride over once in a while, just like I come up here today. What's wrong with that? I'll bet that once Bart gets over this horse, you'll agree that he's all right.'

'How much will you bet?' he laughed.

She stared at him. 'Do you always take people at exactly what they say?'

'Why say something or say anything if you don't mean it?'

She couldn't meet his steady gaze so she looked around at the shed and shack and at the other improvements he had made.

'You've fixed this old place up a lot,' she commented.

'I'd put a new house over there,' he pointed to a piece of land in the crook of the stream. 'You could use this old place for a henhouse.'

'Oh, this place could be made into a nice small stable, too,' she volunteered, closing her eyes and squinting.

'Why, it could be a small stable—I'd never thought of that,' he said.

'I'd like to see a little house nestled in the trees over there, at that,' she mused.

'What time shall I pick you up tomorrow night?' he asked.

'Oh, come early, Jim. The dance starts at eight and it's a long trip to town. Will you ride Silver Cloud?'

He thought he heard a break in her voice.

'Of course I'm not leavin' him for those buzzards to swoop down on.'

'It doesn't matter to me,' she said. Then she quickly added, 'It'll be a wonderful ride down the valley. Some of the people have made the first cut on the hay and the smell is just heavenly. It'll be a wonderful ride back, too, with the moon so big and full. I just love a July moon!'

'Well, I'll be down early. Let me get a saddle on this jughead an' I'll ride you home.'

Walker saddled the stallion and led him out of the corral; Sally recovered her reins and mounted the spirited pinto and waited. Silver Cloud gave several long, leaping bucks as Walker settled himself in the saddle, then he quieted down and they rode down the trail together.

*　　*　　*

Bart Dodge was in a grouchy mood as he lounged on the veranda of the main Pitchfork building. When he had bought the outfit from Almstock, you could sit on the porch and look for miles and nothing but open land met the eye. Now with one thing and another going wrong, all he could see around the place was cattle. No matter what window you looked out you were bound to see a bunch of cows.

In his heart he knew the cowboys that drew his pay were laughing about it; it certainly made their work easier. But the grass was being ruined by the heavy grazing and he worried for fear that even the plentiful water at the ranch could not save him from disaster.

Actually, he didn't see why the cowhands should be amused about the situation, for if he failed they were out of jobs. Apparently, they hadn't considered this. To make matters worse, the price of cattle at the railroad pens in the next county was so low that he could hardly drive them there and break even. In a few months the price of cattle would go up, but how long would he have grass? He couldn't smile and every time he saw somebody around the ranch smiling or joshing, he got furious.

Every time he thought of the foolish statement he had made the day Walker rode Silver Cloud, he grew angrier at his own stupidity. How could the man be so stubborn? Neal Spaker's death meant nothing to Dodge beyond its use to discredit Walker. But even that hadn't worked out because his own riders got hold of the true version via old Ackerman, and now they were more respectful of the lone rancher. Dodge had overheard some of his hands talking and gathered that if they had known the true story they wouldn't have ridden so hard to chase Walker.

Dodge had never been successful at an honest venture and this had not been his first attempt. He had come to the valley with plenty of money. He had bought one of the best ranches; he had increased and improved the stock. For each of the past two years he had been sure that this time he had it made. Ranch profit was good but it was largely nullified by his heavy initial investments. Then several things had gone badly for him. They'd had an open winter, and there was little water runoff into the valley from the higher lands.

First one spring had dried up and then another. Bart had wanted to dynamite the springs because he had seen that method bring them flowing before in other places. His neighbors had advised against this course but he had gone ahead anyhow and dynamited several of his dry springs down the valley from the ranch. The springs were ruined and bone dry until this day.

The year after the springs went dry he had no water problem for it was a rainy summer, but he lost his hay crop. He had planted heavily, hoping to have plenty of fodder on hand the following winter when all the big ranchers would be buying. At that time he had counted on making a deal for water the following year. Then the hay had gone moldy; the whole crop a failure.

The next year was dry again. The coming of the stallion with the run of bad luck had been only a coincidence; he knew this and he held nothing against the horse. In fact the horse had been a source of personal pride, for it was something to own a horse that nobody could ride. He had been falling in debt lately but he still believed some break would change things for him.

His friends in the valley—and he had many—all advised him to reduce his herds and cut his payroll in half but this course of action he adamantly rejected; he would rather watch his resources drain away than give up being the valley's biggest rancher.

His title of captain, of course, was phony. He had used it to introduce himself around Purple Valley when he had come there five years ago with plenty of money. He was good-looking, well-built and had a genial personality that people trusted and liked. Certain of his traits, however, had won him enemies.

Bart's biggest fault, and he admitted this to himself, was that he was lazy; he wanted everything done for him and he didn't keep a close enough check on things that were going on. Further, he was not an experienced rancher and was reluctant to take the advice of his neighbor cowmen. He thought he should be a leader in everything, including giving advice. If he couldn't be the one to give it, he wouldn't take it.

He knew there were a few ways that he could save money but he hated to take the action to put them in effect; it seemed that everything he tried went wrong, so he was reluctant to attempt anything new. Everyone who had talked to him lately had met the same sour mood and this made the men of the valley avoid him all the more. Which naturally made him angrier than ever.

Lash Wade came around the corner and dropped into a chair near him. The foreman started building a cigarette. Although he had arrived with Dodge, he was no partner in the ranch; he had always worked for wages of one kind or another. He had hooked up with Dodge before they came to the valley. Wade had merely grabbed onto Dodge's coattails caring not where the other went but enjoying the reflection of Dodge's flash of greatness.

In spite of the fact that he bore no financial interest in Pitchfork at times he acted as if he were a full partner and this one trait made Dodge hate him.

Bart Dodge knew that if he lost everything he owned in the valley—and at his present rate of losses this was a looming possibility—he knew that Lash Wade would ride out with him as he had come, with nothing but the clothes on his back and the horse he rode. The thought of this made Dodge angry. He had come into the valley with a fortune; now if he lost it he would be riding out on equal terms with Wade whom he had taken care of all these years with the easy job of ramrodding his spread.

He glanced at Wade beside him. He was trying to think of something cutting to say to make Wade uncomfortable.

The foreman scratched his back against the wicker porch chair.

'You've had a tough day, eh, Wade?'

'Who, me? No, I ain't had a tough day,' laughed Wade.

'What's so funny? Why the smile?'

'I always smile—going around with a big sour puss don't solve nothin',' Lash declared.

'I suppose you think I ain't got worries, eh, Lash? You see those cows out there? You know they're eatin' every damn bit of grass we got here?' Dodge's voice rose a tone or two.

'They're sure cuttin' it low to the dirt,' grinned Lash. He smiled because it struck him funny and looking sore or sad wouldn't stop the cattle from grazing.

'That's right. Grin your damn head off but don't do anything about it.'

'Bart, what can I do? Can I make it rain? You say we lose money if we go to market now. Then all we can do is wait and hope to hell it rains soon and fills some of the tanks we dug in the washes. If that happens we may make it through to fall.'

Dodge was silent. He had been thinking hard before Lash had come on the porch. An idea had been taking shape. The events of the past week and the incident of Walker getting his horse had been hammering out an idea within his brain. Now it was taking shape and the more he thought about it the better he liked it. Jim Walker was a symbol he hated. Walker had come to the valley with nothing and yet with each passing season he had increased his stock and holdings, even small as they were. Slowly but surely Walker was carving out a successful career. That was what Dodge had hoped for, ached for, and it didn't seem fair that a loner like Walker should accomplish it. He had been building his plans around Walker and Silver Cloud. He smiled at last and began to build a cigarette.

'Listen Lash.' He smiled pleasantly at the foreman. 'There's something I want you to do. Sally Ackerman's goin' to the dance with Walker, and ...'

CHAPTER TEN

When Walker and the girl rode into the town of Purple and up to the dance hall, Jim was amazed at the number of people present. He estimated that two hundred had already gathered and it was obvious by the great assortment of conveyances that they had come from near and far. There were buggies and four-in-hand coaches. There were spring wagons, buckboards and freight wagons fitted with seats. There were even stage coaches on special runs from other towns.

A dozen picket lines swayed with saddle horses hitched to them, shifting their feet. Half a hundred kerosene lanterns hung on the walls and in the trees to light the outside where barreled beer was being served at a bar made of planks laid across sawhorses. In the empty lot beside the dance hall several barbecue fires were burning as they brought two steers to the culmination of an afternoon's cooking. The heavily spiced smell of the barbecue hung in the air.

Sally had told him how these dances were held twice a year during the haying, one coming early in July and another later in the year if the hay held up. Now the ground of the vacant lot was strewn with freshly cut grass and the smell of the new-mown hay blended with that of the barbecue. Inside the dance hall the band held forth with a noisy blare and through the open window Jim could see a slide trombonist, a piano player, three fiddlers, a cornetist and a drummer all playing feverishly. The beat of feet on the floor rocked the frame building and rolled outside like the distant rumble of thunder. Walker winced when he thought of how many people must be in the room. They were packed in like sardines, and while he didn't relish the thought of being jammed in among them, he did want to feel the girl in his arms.

Sally wore a white riding skirt with a bright red blouse and the scent of her perfume was wonderful to Walker. Their privacy ended with the ride, however, when Jim soon found that she was the most popular girl in the valley, for everyone kept stopping them and talking to her and asking for dances. He heard her promise so many he wondered if one would be left for him. Whenever people came up to them, Walker stepped to the side and listened quietly, seldom speaking as he knew almost no one. He could feel them all staring at him, however, and from time to time he glanced up to see people pointing him out.

The crowd surged from the dance hall as the music stopped and the band climbed out through the window for refreshments. Walker had spent what Sally regarded as a great deal of time in picking the spot where they would leave the horses. Finally he had decided on a well-lighted place near a large oak tree on a rise of ground, so that the horses were a little easier to see from the crowd. Walker kept glancing back, standing on tiptoe at times to make sure the stallion was there.

Over near the barbecue pits someone set off a string of firecrackers and the crowd now surged in that direction.

'Let's go into the dance hall; the band will be back in a minute,' the girl suggested.

Jim led the way, still holding her arm. He could see the jealous glances of some of the younger men who were holding back from approaching the popular girl. Jim knew he was a good deal older than Sally and that she might have had a better time with some of the younger men, but he was determined to frighten off as many of them as possible. As they started to the dance hall, Sheriff Wally Bristol came up. He saw Walker and Sally and stepped toward them.

'Oh hello, Walker. You dance, eh? Hello, Sally.'

She flashed her dazzling smile, and Walker stared fondly at her.

'Listen, Walker,' Bristol said earnestly, 'Dodge and Wade are here tonight. I bet myself a beer that you and Dodge get into some sort of tussle, and that's one bet I sure want to lose. Now you just keep the burrs out of your blanket, will you?'

Walker smiled. 'I'm not looking for any trouble, Sheriff, if that's what you mean.'

'That's exactly what I mean. Say—you didn't ride that silver horse to this shindig, did you?'

'Sure did ride him. I wasn't going to leave

him out in the hills where they could pick him up like a stray. If Dodge wants to prove that he's a horse thief, let him take the horse in front of all these people.'

Jim rose on his toes and glanced toward the oak tree. He could see the diamond blaze and the silver strands of mane he had combed between the stallion's ears. Jim looked back at Bristol. The short sheriff had dashed up the steps of the dance hall and was staring in the direction of Walker's glance until he saw the horse.

Walker led Sally up the steps and Bristol said: 'I shore do hate to see that hoss standin' there like that, Walker. I oughta take him down and put him right into a cell. That hoss is making the air tingle with electricity tonight. You feel it?'

'No,' answered Jim flatly.

'Well, I do an' unless I miss my guess there'll be trouble over that hoss, an' you'll be in it!'

'If there's trouble over the horse, I'll be in it, all right—but I won't start it,' Walker said. As he and Sally were about to enter the hall the sheriff called after them in a loud voice.

'Don't worry about what they said, hitchin' you up with the Wild Bunch, Walker. I sent a telegram, and as far as I could find out you aren't a known member of the gang!'

Walker stopped at the door. The sheriff's remark was like a blow in the back. He had hoped that the talk about his past had stopped when Bristol had laughed it off at Ackerman's ranch a few days before. Now Bristol had carelessly let the remark drop within earshot of a dozen people. And Sally, too, had heard him.

Sheriff Bristol's words sped through the crowd that had been following Sally, then had winged their way among the greater throng, and several of the young men dropped from her cortege. Jim saw the girl glance quickly at him and then away, masking whatever were her thoughts.

The dance hall was unbearably hot, yet the walls were lined with groups of people standing and talking. As Walker and the girl came inside, all heads turned their way. Jim surmised that already word had spread that Bristol thought he might have been one of the Wild Bunch, the gang of feared outlaws from across the Purple Mountains who were a living legend in the valley.

People began to pour into the room and the musicians returned. When they started to play the next number, Walker drew the girl into his arms and slowly waltzed her around the floor. He wasn't a good dancer but he was a willing partner, at least as far as this girl was concerned. He decided upon a course that he would follow and he forced her along his path, first up the room about ten yards and then back the same distance. At each end of the course he

whirled her around so that her back was to the
window and he could look out to make sure the
stallion was still there. She was a strong dancer
and tried to lead him in other directions but he
stubbornly stuck to the path he had chosen and
the other dancers melted out of his way each
time they made the traverse.

Now the musicians started another tune—a
far more lively, spritely piece than the
waltz—and Walker, who had never learned to
dance fast, was left on the sidelines. A young,
dark-haired handsome-looking youngster
whisked Sally around the room like a caroming
rocket. Walker headed toward an open window,
one of the two he had been using to check on
the horse. Abruptly, men who had had enough
fresh air left him the luxury of the whole sill
upon which to sit.

The cool outside air poured into the opening
as a mild breeze came up. Walker, having
assured himself that the stallion was under the
oak tree, enjoyed the coolness and searched the
floor for Sally. She still had the same partner
and they were almost flying with the music by
this time, their feet scarcely touching the floor.
Sally was laughing at something the boy was
saying. The whole scene of the couples enjoying
the swift, graceful dance that Jim was unable to
join, made Walker a little angry. He glimpsed
Sally with her partner and he ran a finger along
the inside of his collar to wipe away

perspiration. The room was hot now, even at the window.

Walker stood up as the dance ended but before Sally could get to him a still livelier piece got possession of the band and they started to swing and sway like things possessed, with the slide trombone screeching and hollering and the cornetist having what appeared to be an epileptic fit, and the drummer went wild. Everyone was shouting and clapping like fools and Walker couldn't see anything to it, but now when he looked up he saw Sally and this time she was with another boy, a sandy-haired cowpuncher he had seen somewhere before.

Apparently they all knew he couldn't dance this fast, new-fangled thing they called ragtime, and they held no fear of him in the throng of wildly racing young people who made up the fast dancers—even if he was an old member of the Wild Bunch.

One dance followed another, each seeming faster than the last, and Walker glanced quickly around, in his growing anger, almost having forgotten the stallion. Silver Cloud was still there, and a couple of old timers were standing up close and admiring his fine points while they sipped their beer. Outside under the trees a group had gathered, singing songs and swaying to the music of their harmonicas and squeeze boxes. Walker wished he were among them instead of in the hot dance hall; then the slow music of a waltz brought him back to the room and he started off the window sill.

Jim Walker longed to dance with the girl again. Now as he stepped forward to meet her, the smiling face of Bart Dodge appeared out of the crowd. The rancher was dressed to the nines, as usual. The range king of the valley shouldered his way through the crowd.

'Just a minute, Walker,' he called in his deep baritone voice. 'You may have won my best horse, but you can't have every dance with a sweet, popular girl like Sally, here. I spoke for the next waltz and the lady promised it to me.' Smiling, he swept her into his arms and they glided away through the crowd.

Jim stood awkwardly by the window with his hand still outstretched, his face red. Someone near him on the sidelines whispered something that brought a giggle. His eyes followed the perfect flowing movement of Dodge and Sally for a moment and he grudgingly had to admit that the Pitchfork owner was a much better dancer than he could ever be. He went back to staring glumly out the window; the stallion was still there, but he found himself wishing he hadn't come to the dance at all.

He scarcely knew the music had stopped when Sally was at his side and holding his arm. She looked up into his face. The sudden closeness of her and the warmth of her body made him forget all his bitter thoughts, and he couldn't help smiling at her.

'Hello, stranger,' he greeted.

'Hi!' she laughed. 'Golly, let's go outside for awhile, Jim. It's about time for the barbecue.'

'Well, I guess I can eat a lot better than I can dance fast,' he grinned as they pushed through the crowd and went outside. Already people had started to line up for the barbecue.

Lash Wade was standing near the building with a small knot of men around him. The Pitchfork foreman looked up when he saw Jim and Sally coming into the yard.

'Let's get something to drink,' said Jim.

'All right; I am thirsty,' she answered.

They headed for the drink stand. A burly, black-bearded man stood in their path, and Walker suddenly realized that the man had been dogging them all evening. First he had been near them in the yard and then later Jim had seen him in the dance hall. Now he was coming purposefully toward them, a frown on his brow, his elbows crooked belligerently.

CHAPTER ELEVEN

Jim swung Sally to the side to avoid what seemed to be an inevitable collision with the heavy-set, stubble-jawed cowboy.

'Hey, you, Walker, hold on a minute. I want

to say a word to you,' bellowed the thickset giant.

They stopped and waited.

'You're the galoot that rode that silver horse, ain't you?' He was closer now and Walker saw that his coarse black hair seemed to grow almost down to his eyes. The man's low forehead now wrinkled like a washboard. He was dressed in grimy overalls and a sweat-stained red bandanna gave his outfit the only bit of color. He wore a bone-handled revolver at his belt along with a sheathed hunting knife. He was clearly out of place in this crowd of peaceful ranch people, and he had received many a wondering glance from them.

'I don't know you,' Walker began, 'so I don't see what—'

'Just a minute, buster. Don't get previous with Sam Parker, son, or I'll teach you a damn good lesson. Is that yore hoss over there—the one with the mane like wire silver? Just you answer me that question.'

The crowd started building up around them for the loud, bullying tones of Parker were audible to everyone in the lot. And Sally, too, did her share in drawing the crowd because she was so beautiful and popular, and because a full two dozen young men had commenced hating Walker for no other reason than that he seemed to be, at the moment, her favorite.

Also, there was the mention of Silver Cloud.

101

The animal had drawn the attention of a hundred men already on this night. Anyone who hadn't heard about his breaking by Walker was quickly led past for a look at the stallion. As there were many older men who were more interested in horses than in dancing, Silver Cloud was the most popular celebrity present, and a constant stream of earnest admirers of horseflesh had wound their way about the magnificent horse.

Aside from Parker's loud, harsh voice there was an air of mystery about the man. He had never been seen in the valley before this and all were wondering what he was doing here and from where he had come. His appearance was so out of key with the celebrating crowd that many a man hoped he would soon go on his way. His appraisal of the women had been bold and frank and while his glances were unanimously ignored by them, no man had stepped forth to take issue with the insolent intruder.

With the wrath of the man now centered on Walker, the curious were eager to watch the stout man more closely and the crowd closed about the three like a human wall.

Walker frowned at the closely packed onlookers. He could see the grinning faces of many men, most of them eager for his downfall. Jim realized that to ride a horse that had never been ridden was one thing, but to come to the dance with a popular girl like Sally was another. While riding the horse had made him a sort of hero to some, coming with the girl had made him an enemy to others.

'I know you, Parker; I remember you now,' Walker said, his voice so low that the people in the crowd strained for every word.

'Sure you know me,' roared Parker, laughing. 'You got my hoss, Walker. Silver Cloud is my hoss an' I aim tuh take him back to Star Valley!'

The crowd absorbed this as a murmur swept through their ranks about Parker's intention. Jim glanced at Sally apologetically and shrugged.

'I'm sorry,' he began.

'Shut up yore palaver with that she-male, Walker. If you wanta talk to her, save it, 'cause I'm takin' my hoss and goin'. If you got any objections you better mouth 'em right quick. A Mex stole the hoss from me an' I been trailin' him for years, an' now I find you've got the hoss. That hoss had three small notches in his right ear.' Parker paused and glanced around at the crowd. He added: 'Somebody look and see if that ain't so.'

Shuffling footsteps in the crowd nearest the horse indicated an eager response to Parker's request.

'That's right!' shouted a voice. 'Three notches on his right ear.'

'Three notches—okay,' came a second voice.

'Why, that don't mean a damn thing,' declared Walker, suddenly on the defensive and looking around for support. He added quickly, 'Somebody get Sheriff Bristol over here!'

'He's up at the jail lockin' up one of Bart Dodge's boys that got drunk,' shouted a man.

'Well, somebody run and get him,' answered Walker looking at the sea of faces and searching for someone he knew.

'Whatsa matter, you afraid of this guy, Walker?' came a shout.

'I never see a hoss thief that wasn't scared when the time come to own up,' loudly declared Sam Parker. He stepped menacingly forward.

Jim shoved Sally gently toward the crowd which absorbed her into its ranks; she disappeared from his gaze.

'Listen, Parker,' he entreated, 'just because you know that horse has three notches on his ear don't mean nothin' to me. You could have learned that from Bart Dodge. I won that horse from Dodge fair and square and you can ask anybody here!'

Sam Parker grinned and turned to the crowd for verification.

'Aw, Walker was just bein' a stubborn fool. He ain't got no legal hold on that hoss,' grumbled a man whose face Walker could not see.

The remark brought a shout of laughter and

Jim's face turned a fiery red. He glowered at the crowd and Parker.

'All right, Parker. That horse is mine. If you want him, you can start in by killin' me.' His voice ended in a shout.

'I know you, Walker,' laughed Parker. 'You'll not get me to pull iron on you. They still remember you over in Star Valley.' Parker glanced around at the crowd. The second mention of Star Valley, notorious as an outlaw hangout, brought a murmur from the onlookers as the words of Parker were passed along.

'You can't walk in here and call me a horse thief just because you once owned this horse, Parker. What about Dodge—he owned the horse before I did. And somebody owned the horse before Dodge. You gonna stand here and call everybody that owned this horse a thief? Why, you've got no claim on this horse at all. Now stand out of my way. If you still think this horse is yours, go see Sheriff Bristol.'

'You sure are anxious to see the sheriff,' drawled Parker. 'I remember the time when a sheriff was just somethin' you looked at over your shoulder or maybe once in awhile in a gun-sight. Haw! Haw!'

The remark brought a shout of laughter.

'That's a dirty lie, Parker,' shouted Jim.

'Take off your gun an' we'll see if it's the truth. I'll beat the truth out of you, Walker.'

Walker unbuckled his gun slowly and

watched as Parker did the same. Jim handed the shell belt and holster to someone in the crowd near him. Parker just let his fall in the dirt and closed with a rush, his head down.

Walker sidestepped and brought his fist down with all his might on the back of Parker's head, knocking the bully into the dust. Parker dug his hands into the dirt and came up crouching, fists closed. He circled, laughing. Jim circled the other way. Parker let fly a handful of dirt at Walker's head but the other sidestepped and the crowd got it instead. Again Parker made one of his bull-like, head-down charges and a segment of the crowd melted, pushing, shoving and trampling one another.

Jim jumped aside again, aiming a blow at the big man's head but one of the outspread arms hooked him around the waist and carried him to the ground with a crash. Parker laughed wildly. Suddenly the heavier man was all over him, his huge arms clubbing and numbing Walker as Jim struggled to get on top. Even the mere movements of the man's arms felt like hammer blows to Jim and for a second his vision clouded with pain.

Parker dumped a handful of sand in Jim's eyes, then with a hard, heavy palm he scoured the gritty stuff into Walker's face, making the rancher roar in pain as the harsh abrasive cut into his features. He felt his lip rolled back from his teeth and his nose twisted at the nostrils. He could hear Parker laughing insanely but he could see nothing but red. Blinded by the sand, he flailed out with his arms and legs trying to hurt the heavy man who was now sitting on his chest.

Nothing could move the bulk of Parker. Jim guessed that the man was twice his weight. He felt another handful of sand hit his face and he could hear the crowd yelling angrily at Parker but they were doing nothing. He felt thick, heavy fingers probing for his eyes, trying to gouge them out.

With every bit of his strength he wriggled and squirmed to get out from under Parker; it was no use, the man had mutilated men in this manner before and he was going to do it again now. As he wriggled Parker slid one hand up to grab and hold him by the hair. With the other hand he continued to pull and gouge at Walker's features.

Jim found that his own blows merely rained off Parker's arms, arms so thick and muscular that his fists felt as if they were landing on fence posts. He groped for Parker's face but the man increased the pressure on Jim's scalp and he had to reach for the hand that was entwined in his hair.

Parker grabbed another handful of dirt and growled at the crowd as somebody yelled something at him. The crowd was spellbound, powerless to interfere. Parker ground a huge handful of the dirt into Jim's mouth and as he did Walker brought his teeth down hard and clamped them on two of Parker's fingers.

Parker screamed with pain and loosened his grip on Jim's scalp, but his hand shot to Jim's throat in an attempt to throttle the twisting Walker. The pain was too great, however, and his hand shot upward and started to knead at Walker's jaw hinge.

Walker ground his teeth into the two fingers with all the savagery of a wild animal. He felt the flesh part and the blood spurt into his mouth. He ground his teeth through the bone and felt the bruiser's weight rise from his body, hearing Parker's howl of rage and pain.

Parker lunged upward, believing that his movement would make Walker lose his grip but instead he merely increased the pain in his hand, for Walker's teeth did not release the fingers. Jim found himself being jerked up to his knees and he rose the rest of the way, swinging viciously, the blows cutting at Parker's face.

Jim's jaws had been locked in agony a moment before with the pain from the dirt rubbed into his eyes, nose and mouth. When his jaws released their grip Parker looked at his hand and uttered a horrified cry. One of his fingers was hanging by a mere thread of skin.

Parker grabbed his injured right hand, his eyes rolling in fear, but there was no escape from the tight circle of the crowd. The savage combat was making the onlookers like animals as they shouted for their favorite.

Walker staggered back, rubbing at his eyes; he blinked hard and found he could see the fear-crazed face of Parker as the man clutched his crippled hand and tried to get through the crowd. The men on the edge were now taunting him, whereas moments before even the sight of Parker had cowed most of them. Now they wouldn't let him escape from the circle, though he kept shouting for a doctor as he tried to hold his severed finger in place.

Walker rushed up from behind and grabbed him by his long hair. Parker let out a scream as Jim jerked him over backward and slammed his knee against Parker's backbone. Parker gasped and went down and Jim drove his boot into the man's bulky ribs. It was a savage no-holds-barred fight and Jim knew that to give quarter now could mean his death. There were only two things that could save him, lick the bully or have Bristol arrive. The savage, howling crowd wouldn't take a hand. He mustn't let the heavy man get a grip on him again for if he did the man would kill him or gouge out his eyes.

Walker felt his strength fading, and he stomped at the face of Parker. Parker threw up a hand and caught the boot. He started dragging himself to his feet again and Walker hit him in the face, only to find Parker's steely grip close about his wrist. In the crowd he heard a girl scream as Parker grappled and increased his hold, bearing Jim once more to the ground. He felt the heavy bulk of Parker fall with crushing power against him, driving the breath from his body. And then suddenly Parker seemed to float in the air as if by magic.

Through his bleary eyes Walker looked upward and could see the grim visage of Wally Bristol standing over him, his fist wrapped around a wagon spoke. Apparently, the sheriff had buffaloed Parker with the club, and just in time. Jim sat up and rubbed his hands at his eyes.

CHAPTER TWELVE

Jim pulled himself slowly to his feet. When Bristol had pushed his way through the crowd and slugged Parker with the heavy wooden spoke the crowd started to dissolve. With the arrival of the law the fun was over and dance music was enticing the crowd back into the hall.

Sally was at his side now, leading him toward a water barrel. Jim plunged his arms into the cool water up to his elbows and splashed the soothing water onto his face. He rinsed it again and again, trying to keep his eyes open so as to clean them as well as possible. Finally he looked around and saw several men grinning at him.

There was nothing derisive in the smiles but he ignored them nevertheless; people had ignored him when he needed them. Now he didn't need them, any of them. He turned and looked at the girl. He could see the compassion and fright in her eyes as she viewed his cleansed face. He could feel his torn lips still bleeding inside his mouth. His eyes ached from the sand, but he felt better. He knew he must be a sight for washing away the dirt had left the bruises, scratches and cuts fully exposed.

'Golly, Jim, I think I better take you over to the doc and have him look at your lip,' she said, her voice concerned.

'I'm all right; let's go home,' he mumbled.

'No, you ain't all right,' said Sheriff Wally Bristol, coming up to them. 'For one thing you're gettin' set to go home without yore gun. Here, put it on. Steer clear of that black-bearded bum that I clubbed off yore back. He's over there somewhere rubbin' his head. I give him fifteen minutes to light a shuck out of here!'

'Thanks, Bristol. You got there just in time 'cause I couldn't have stood up much longer,' Jim admitted.

'You did all right, son, and you surprised a few people, I think. I'm goin' into the dance hall. You two all right?'

111

'Good night, Sheriff, and thanks so very much,' said Sally.

Jim buckled the Colt on and looked at the girl, sorry that he had to be the cause of ruining her evening. He wanted to get out of the town, but he hesitated and asked: 'Would you like to have some barbecue? I don't think I could eat anything but I sure could drink a barrel!'

'Jim, are you sure you're all right? I hate to keep you here. I'd like to fix your face, if I could. Let's get something to drink, anyway.'

They headed toward the counter where liquid refreshment was being served. The thought of the stallion suddenly occurred to Walker and he whirled to check on the horse. Apparently the fight had addled his senses more than he had realized, for he looked right past the spot where the horse should be and on down the line. Then remembering that the horse was back under the tree he swung his glance there, but the stallion was gone.

For one terrible moment he hoped that the horse had lowered his head to graze but then he saw the gap in the line and realized that the fight had been staged to cover up the theft of his horse. Dodge had cleverly duped him into fighting the big Parker and now the stallion was probably being led by fast riders to some hiding place in the valley.

'My horse!' he yelled at the top of his lungs.

Everyone turned and looked at him.

'They got my horse!' he shouted, running toward the spot where Silver Cloud had been picketed. He grabbed a man and shook him by the shoulder. 'They stole my horse! Can't you see they stole my horse? They used the fight to get him.' He whirled around and ran to another man. 'You see who got my horse?'

'Why, I was watching the fight,' said the man. He began to laugh. 'Don't get so excited—maybe your hoss just came unhitched.'

'Unhitched, hell! I tell you, Bart Dodge stole him. He—'

'That's crazy,' said another man. 'Dodge was up to the jail tryin' to bail out his rider. He couldn't 'a' done it.'

Jim pushed the man rudely aside and raced for the horses. Some of the men ran after him but he easily outdistanced them. He jumped under the line near where the stallion had been tied with the pinto. A gun flashed near him and a shot rang out. He slid to the ground, drawing his own gun. For a moment he was sure that someone had shot at him. He fired and a figure dodged into the trees and disappeared into the shadows. Jim jumped up to pursue him and fell headlong over a body on the ground. He scrambled around and started to roll the form he had tripped on. Even before he saw the face he knew he was dealing with the bulk of Sam Parker.

Just as he rolled Parker over, some men who had been following him rushed upon the scene. Jim looked at the chest of Parker where blood was pouring forth. The man was dead, shot through the heart.

Jim stood as the men ran up.

'Somebody shot him,' murmured Jim. He holstered his own gun and the men looked at him with curious glances.

'Yeah, that somebody wouldn't be you, would it, Walker? This makes two men you've killed over that horse,' said one of the men.

'I didn't shoot this man,' Jim said quickly. 'I ran over here and somebody shot him just the minute I ran up. I saw the flash, although Parker was already on the ground. I fired a shot at somebody running into the trees over there. Go over if you don't believe me. You should find tracks.'

'Yeah, a fine lot o' tracks we'd see!' laughed one of the men.

'Only been a hundred hosses over that ground tonight!' said another.

Walker realized that they were right; it would be impossible to single out any track from the field which had been ground to a finely pulverized dust by all the traffic.

'Somebody get the sheriff. I ain't gonna make any citizen's arrest in this case,' said a tall fellow.

The men stared coldly at Jim and, with a

114

sinking feeling in the pit of his stomach, Walker realized he had been judged guilty by these men. Moreover, they could probably call themselves witnesses, since they had arrived on the scene so quickly.

Jim's Colt appeared in his hand again and the men blinked as he said: 'All right, boys, you don't sound like you'd be friendly witnesses to me. I'll just grab a horse and slide out of here.' Walker backed down the line of horses.

'Hey!' one of the men shouted in the direction of the dance hall. 'Over here—it's that murderin' skunk, Jim Walker. He just shot the guy he fought with. Hurry!'

The sound of running feet had already come to Walker long before the man had yelled out. It had taken the crowd a moment to realize that the explosions had come from a Colt, for large firecrackers had been going off all night. The men had twisted their heads this way and that, trying to discern the direction. Then, with the shout, they poured toward the horses. The music stopped and the muffled roar of feet shuffling and running across the board floor echoed outside.

Above all of the noise and confusion, the voice of Sheriff Wally Bristol shouted for law and order. Walker raced along the line of horses. As long as he was going to be a horse thief, he decided he'd be a good one. He dashed down the line, looking them over—pintos,

115

roans, chestnuts, sorrels, duns, bays and piebalds, and mixtures of them all. A giant bay fidgeted as he ran past and he turned to give the big hunter a second glance. The horse turned his head as far as the hitch would permit and gave Jim a wild eye-rolling look of panic.

The horse was over seventeen hands and his head was up, his ears perked forward until it seemed they would touch the lower limbs of the oak he was under. Jim ran in beside him and jerked the reins loose. They were coming now, a hundred boots thudding on the earth, with women screaming in the background. He smiled grimly as a running man passed him, not seeing him between the horses and in the shadows.

He kept talking to the fidgety horse while he got his toe in the stirrup. He swung up and held his breath, hoping the cinch was tight. It was, and he backed the horse out of the line.

'There he is!' they shouted.

The bay gave a tremendous jump as Jim spurred him hard and lashed his rump with the long reins. Walker dashed him down the row of horses and around the corner. As they raced along the street he could see people rushing out the dance hall's big double doors. Some shots rang out, but none of the bullets came close. Everyone was afraid of hitting someone else so the guns were aimed high.

He raced down the main street and out the

valley road. Before he passed the last house he could hear the rumble of horsemen behind him. The bay could run like the wind and he wryly congratulated himself on his choice of horseflesh. For the time being, Silver Cloud was something he could not afford to think about; the men on his trail were after him for murder and they had rope with them. He had a long ride ahead before he could reach the part of the valley where a man could hide, and before he could make it, they might have him. If so, he was a goner, for by his running he tacitly had admitted his guilt. Yet, to stay might have been as bad; he was glad he was alive, even if running. The wind felt good on his bruised and battered face.

He stuck to the valley road and looking back he saw the riders turn the corner coming out of town. They were leaning far forward in their saddles, urging their mounts to top speed. At least fifty horsemen turned the corner and Walker still couldn't believe that they all were hunting him. They swept along in a huge group keeping him in sight but not sprinting to get him. The heavy rumble of their hoofbeats rolled down the road behind him.

He was gaining rapidly on them so he slowed the bay and then he could hear the angry shouts as the men denounced him; they had hoped he would run the bay hard and then be unable to hold them off when they pressed him. They spurted ahead, increasing their pace and so he increased his accordingly. They slowed from a gallop to a lope and Walker did the same, although he found it the horse's worst gait. They gained rapidly on him and he looked back in alarm when a rifle bullet sang past his head. It was obvious that the owner of the bay was riding in the pursuit because the group stuck to the lope and continued to gain with each mile.

Whoever owned the horse, he reasoned, knew that the animal was a poor runner at a lope so Walker changed back to a smooth, unspurred gallop and started to widen the gap again. Some horses, he knew, could gallop all night but could kill themselves if they loped for an hour. Other horses could walk so fast that they would hold another horse in a half-trot and in a day's walk would kill the animal in the partial trot. Every horse was different; the best ground-gaining of the bay was at the gallop and it seemed to be less tiring to him than the lope, so Walker avoided the other gait and pulled away.

He could hear the cry of dismay from the rider in the rear as he used the gallop to pull completely away. There were few courses open to him and he wondered which would be the best. To keep on going down the valley meant that he would have to pass close to the Dodge ranch and there was always the chance that Pitchfork riders would ride out and intercept him.

He could head for his own place and pick up supplies, but that would be risky, too; no matter how much of a lead he built up, the posse could shrink it fast if they figured he was heading for his place and likely to stop there. Then, too, he didn't want to risk the chance that they might burn his place down out of frustration at not getting him. He knew that even if Sheriff Bristol was heading the posse the lawman would have a hard time holding down the many hotheads in such a large group.

He didn't want to go near the Ackermans' place, even though he knew old Ackerman was there and would likely lend him a fresh horse. The rest of the valley was open land and there was no place to hide. There was but one refuge, and that was the Purples. In the wild country of the mountains he had at least a chance to give his pursuers the slip. He had no intention at the moment of leaving the country. He was positive that after things cooled down he could send a message to Bristol; he had faith that the little lawman would hear his story, for the sheriff seemed to like him.

It was late when he brought the bay past Ackerman's ranch and he thought about Sally. What would she think of him, running away like that? Would she understand, or would she blame him? By the stars he figured it was close to one o'clock in the morning. He could see the lighted windows in the cabin as the old man waited up for him and the girl to return. Well, Jim wouldn't be seeing Sally home tonight. Jim cursed himself for taking the girl to the dance; he should have known that he couldn't go without getting into trouble.

He glanced back, and through the bright moonlight he saw that half the horsemen had dropped by the wayside or turned back. The bay had set a grueling pace down the valley, and more than one posseman who thought he was setting out for a short burst of riding and a triumphant return, with the culprit on the end of a rope and a share in the glory, had become discouraged with the steady pounding of the saddle.

Past Ackerman's he turned off the road and heard the others shout and slant off after him. He headed for a wild stretch of mountain country that would be hard on the men following him, but it would be almost as hard on himself and his horse.

CHAPTER THIRTEEN

As he approached the mountains the posse closed the gap with a rush. Now more than ever they wanted to keep him in sight for they realized that their horses would have a good chance to rest after they hit the more rugged country, where even Jim Walker would have to go slowly.

Jim looked back and cursed as he watched them gain in an all-out effort to shrink the distance. Wally Bristol was in the lead by a good two lengths and his toasted sorrel was a magnificent mount, a thoroughbred all the way, that had never once dropped from the lead. Bristol bore along in front with the brim of his hat blown back by the wind. The sheriff was a fearful sight because he seemed relentless, his posture never stooped or sagged. He just kept coming on, his body appearing one with that of the sorrel.

Jim led the horse into the first jumble of boulders and disappeared from sight. As he did so there was a shout from the twenty-odd horsemen who still dogged his trail. The bay scrambled over the rocky surface and Walker glanced back to see how badly the animal's shoes were marking the rock. They would be able to see his tracks in a few hours and then they could trail him. For the time being, with the blackness that comes before dawn on his side, they would have to follow a blind trail or stop altogether. He heard them drawing rein to stop.

Sunrise found Walker deep in the mountains; unfortunately this was strange territory to him, and he soon realized that if he had gone farther back along the valley and closer to his own ranch, he would have had a better chance of dodging the pursuit. Now he could see why wise Wally Bristol had not bothered to follow him more closely, but had stopped to rest. There was only one direction Jim could go—follow the sheer sixty-foot-deep canyon of Almstock Creek that wound through that part of the mountains. To stay in the good cover he was forced to take the edge of the gorge. There was no place to cross the canyon for miles.

Bristol, an old timer in the valley, naturally knew this and he rested his men and horses, then made up for lost time at daylight. His men rode quickly in the light and could easily see Walker's trail where the iron horseshoes had marred the granite and shale. Walker had picked his trail slowly in the dark, as he was uncertain of the country and wary of the treacherous gorge with its many cutoffs.

An hour after dawn Walker looked back and saw them winding around a narrow ledge where he had passed not long before. They sighted him just as he disappeared behind a gigantic boulder and he heard their glad shout. They had had two or three hours' rest whereas he was exhausted from riding all night and ready to drop from the saddle.

Now the tense, seesaw chase began in earnest. The bay still went wonderfully on; true, the pace was slow but the footing was more important for the animal was tired, exhausted. Once he had an open stretch to pass through and the men in pursuit had dropped from their horses and fired with rifles at rest. Another second and they would have had his range before he got the bay into cover. Walker looked back and wiped his brow. Another open stretch and they might not even get to question him; these men were shooting to kill.

Thirty feet across, the canyon was far too wide to jump and even in the narrower places there was no place to start the horse for a take-off. As he went higher, which he had to do with the pressure of the pursuit, the gorge grew deeper. Now it was a full eighty feet to the bottom where Almstock Creek beat its torturous course of boiling fury through the canyon floor.

He had never heard of the bridge, but his heart leaped at the distant sight of it.

Across there on the other side, he could lose himself for a year from the greatest posse of trackers in the world, for there lay the wild country leading right up to the peaks of the Purples with Glass Mountain in the background. Thousands of square miles of desolate land, populated only by mountain lion, bear and other wild game. Here was a hunter's paradise and the canyon had cut him off from it. The posse was but a quarter-mile behind him and only the slippery going along the rocky, narrow trail edging the gorge kept them at bay.

Any moment they might gain enough distance to put a bullet through his back, and Walker had the uncomfortable feeling that they'd be glad to do it. Just ahead of him the trail swung out on a narrow outcropping and he pushed the bay around the corner slowly, awaiting his first close glimpse of the bridge that he had sighted. Then his heart sank. Immediately he looked back to see if his pursuers had come into view. There would be that moment when they also could see the bridge, and see him as well.

There was no point in hesitating, for the bridge was a bitter joke of fate, an ancient structure built by some trapper or woodsman of the fur-trading days and only for foot traffic. The rickety structure spanned a narrow portion of the canyon where the upper walls leaned together and then fell sickeningly inward to widen at the bottom. In length, the flimsy span was not over fifteen feet, but it was rotten with age. Two long logs formed the main beams. These were pocketed with rot and fungus and green mold covered the north side. At the near edge of the canyon one big log was almost rotted away where it rested on the canyon's edge.

Across the two main logs were a series of smaller logs, four or five inches in diameter, which had been notched and laid side by side to

124

make a crude flooring. The width of the bridge was two feet or less and a rickety, rotten railing spanned either side. The railing on the south had fallen so that it pointed prophetically down into the depths of the gorge. Many of the cross logs had rotted and fallen completely away and several were broken; the bark had peeled away years before and now only a gray, dry-rotted exterior met the eye.

A wild idea struck Walker. He knew the bay was sure-footed; that much he had already seen, so why not try him at the bridge? What had he to lose? It was only a matter of time until he'd probably be shot or lynched, anyway. And still he knew of the great ability of a horse to find sure and safe footing where treachery prevailed and if ever there was treachery it was in the rotten wood of the bridge. If he left the horse and wriggled across on his belly, then the posse could follow the same way. And they soon would hunt him down because they would have the advantage of numbers, but if he once got into the wild country with a horse, who would dare to follow?

Grinning, Walker jumped from the saddle and twisted off the one remaining rail, it fell discouragingly easily and he watched it spiral down carrying one of the uprights. It hit the water and was lost in the foam for an instant, then reappeared only to be dashed against the rocks and smashed to bits. He tentatively tried the cross boards with his hands; they seemed stronger than they looked.

Walker found the stirrup and stepped onto the horse just as the first of the posse swung into view around the outcropping. He heard their shouts above the roar of the creek below; now was the time when they could easily get him with a rifle. He looked back and found they were sitting their saddles watching him, spellbound. The main body was still out of sight; only Wally Bristol and some of the men were visible. They did not try to shoot as Walker started the horse toward the narrow footbridge.

The bay whickered nervously but he seemed to know what was ahead of him. He pawed at the rotten wood with a hoof and did a little half-step as he approached the narrow strand. As Walker encouraged him, he placed his weight on the first boards. They held. Another shout came from down-canyon; men were yelling at him to stop. Evidently there were those in the party who knew the condition of the bridge.

Walker tried not to look down. The horse was fully as wide as the bridge, so he had little view of the rickety structure below him. Far down he could see the rapids and whirlpools churning and leaping in a white, foam-frothed dance. Vapor hung heavily in the air above the turbulent water so that it seemed as if one were looking down into a cloudy abyss. The bay refused two of the boards, and tentatively placed a forehoof farther on, seeking more solid timber. They were halfway over, and now there could be no turning back. Walker knew that the slightest lurch would send them crashing through the rotted flooring to death on the glistening black rocks below.

Then his heart drove into his throat like an arrow thudding home. The forefoot of the bay crashed through the timber and the animal balanced precariously for a second on three legs. This was it, for if one more hoof went through the horse would be helpless. The bay started to tremble as he realized his predicament. Slowly he raised the hoof and felt ahead. He had footing and went forward another step. Walker heard a cheer and looked back, amazed.

Wally Bristol and the others were watching his desperate gamble and they were thrilled enough to let him have his chance. Or was it that they were so certain that he would never make it and would save the cost of his trial by plummeting to his death a hundred feet below? At any rate, they did nothing to worsen the odds against him. As men of the West, they admired him for his nervy thousand-to-one gamble, and were giving him this one impossible chance, with his life now hanging on the sure-footedness and instinct of the bay.

Walker felt a trickle of cold sweat run down the middle of his back. Then his heart surged into his throat again as the bay's back foot broke through the bridge. The horse hung still, poised delicately on three hoofs and Walker felt the chill of panic. The horse and himself weighed well over a thousand pounds and every time the animal threw all his weight on three feet for a long interval like this, it meant that the weight was divided by three instead of four. The pressure was over three hundred pounds per hoof. And the sharp horseshoes were liable to slice through the rotted logs at any second.

As the back hoof went through the flooring, there arose a desperate cry down the gorge from the watching cowboys and sheriff. The bay inched forward until it was but a foot from the far side. One front hoof found the rock and the horse stepped lightly ahead, only to sink through with a rear hoof. Walker slid forward in the saddle, and keeping as much weight on the forequarters of the horse as he could, he let himself slide down around the bay's neck. Then he felt the wonderful relief of having the canyon rim solidly beneath his feet.

Walker tried to lead the horse forward, but the bad log gave way and both its back feet slipped through. The bay lurched backward. It would be doubly tragic to lose the horse now, Walker realized. The bay's doubled rear knee now rested on solid wood, but the other leg pointed down into the gorge. The horse was rocked back at a bad angle, and Walker pulled mightily on the reins. Reaching over, he clutched a handful of mane. Jim was so terrified by the thought that the animal would be lost, after coming this close to making it across, that for a moment he had the wild idea of pulling back the horse if he fell. He kept telling himself to be ready to let go the mane. The horse's eyes mirrored pure terror as he struggled frantically, then, in a climactic effort, he lurched free of the hole. And Jim Walker was yelling and sobbing for joy as he led the horse into the jumble of rocks beyond. He heard some one behind let out a glad shout and he smiled in gratitude to think of the break they had given him.

In the safety of the rocks, Walker quickly pulled the saddle from the bay and started to wipe off the sweat with the saddle blanket. He hobbled the animal and left him to rest while he crawled to the edge of the boulders and watched the bridge, thinking: Let them try and cross now, by any means. From his position he could hold back an army. The long column of tired riders hove into view and Jim could hear them talking plainly. Bristol rode beyond the approach of the bridge and dismounted; several of the men, obviously the main leaders, crawled from the saddle. Most of the men wearily sat their horses and stared glumly at the bridge.

'I never see the like o' that,' said Bristol,

shaking his head.

'We should have shot him,' protested one of the men.

'Why didn't you shoot him, Bill?' asked Bristol, his eyes twinkling.

'Hell, I held my fire because I swore he'd never make it across. I still don't believe he rode his horse across that pile of dry rot!'

'Well, let's not palaver all day. Let's get across there after him,' Bristol said.

'Go across there? Not me, Sheriff. I ain't no tightroper. I'll shut my eyes and ride along these thousand-foot-high canyon walls, but I don't cross that bridge. Not afoot nor ahorseback. My Gawd!'

'That goes double for me,' declared another. 'How do we know he ain't waitin' in them rocks—how'd you like to belly-crawl part way out on that wreck and then have some joker start makin' it jiggle and sway with a Colt? I'll do my swingin' home on the porch hammock! It's only a two-foot fall off that.'

The men started laughing and nodding agreement at the same time.

'We get over there on foot, and he'll sashay away on that bay. What kind of a race would that be?' argued another.

'There isn't enough good timber on this side to build a replacement, either,' observed Bristol, shrugging.

'I don't think we want to catch the damn

fool, anyhow. He won me over when he pulled that hoss through, and I made up my mind he was innocent when I see that,' declared a fat man, still mounted.

'That was a helluva trick, all right,' grinned another of the posse. 'I kinda got to likin' him myself, even though he has broke my hind quarters so that I'll never want to sit again. I reckon he had his trial out there on that bridge, and somebody bigger than me—did the judgin'.'

'Well, from the sound of you,' began Wally Bristol, 'you're all saying let's go home, that right? I agree he's got a style for pullin' the damndest things. I'm for ridin' for breakfast and forgettin' the whole damn thing till he shows up somewhere. Like you say, he could hole out in the mountains till winter if he had a mind to.'

Bristol mounted and led out the discouraged posse.

CHAPTER FOURTEEN

Jim Walker watched the last horseman fade from sight as the posse of riders slowly wound along the treacherous trail. As the last hunch-shouldered, weary horseman passed from view, he sighed and turned to gaze fondly at the horse; minutes before when he had been rubbing the sweat from the bay he had noticed the Window Sash brand on the animal's rear flank.

The Window Sash outfit was owned by the Weavers and Jim grimly reckoned that he had added that family to his growing list of enemies. He doubted that any other horse, of all those at the hitch line the night before, could have crossed the rotted bridge or run as well as had the bay. He owed the horse his life, but he resolved somehow to return the animal to the Weaver ranch when he could.

He finished rubbing down the horse and then looked to his own comfort. Physically he was exhausted but he didn't like their position because they were too close to the bridge. He led the horse into a more wild and tangled area about a mile and a half farther on. Here he found a small grassy meadow and he hobbled the bay and stretched out on the ground to sleep. He reasoned that even if the posse thought to fool him and sneak back around the canyon to pick up his trail, they still would have to cover a distance that would take them into darkness.

It was unlikely that they would try this. They were, for the most part, glory-seekers and—with the exception of Wally Bristol—there wasn't a man among them that Walker would have feared to have on his trail. They had no supplies and would have to depend for meals upon the people whose ranches they passed. He knew that few ranchers would welcome the job of providing a meal for so big a group. He was sure that if Bristol was going to continue to trail him, he would return to Purple and get rid of the present posse. In its place he would mount one or two good trackers, men who could live in the wild places without having to burden themselves with a lot of supplies. Then they would come back to the bridge and pick up the trail.

Jim awoke under the strong sun of late afternoon. He sat up, looked around and rubbed his day's growth of stubbly whiskers. He was stiff and lame from the long ride of the night before. The bay had wandered to the edge of the meadow and was grazing contentedly.

Walker got up and limped slowly toward a heavy growth of trees that bordered the meadow. He disappeared into the woods and the bay lifted his head and watched curiously as he munched the grass. Walker was not gone long when three shots punctuated the stillness and again the bay horse stared toward the woods. Walker came through the trees with two quail. He had found them roosting and shot off their heads.

Jim built a fire, cleaned the birds, and then roasted the bits of flesh separately over the flame on green sticks. He ate slowly licking his lips and savoring the tenderness of the unseasoned meat. When he was finished his hunger was somewhat satisfied. Although he had been turning his plight over in his mind, he still hadn't decided what he should do next. He was worried about his own place and particularly about the stock; he hoped that old Ackerman, after Sally had told what had happened, would take care of things.

Of course, too, he worried that they might think him guilty of murdering Parker, and so not worthy of their help. It had all happened so fast. He was not even sure what Sally would think. He knew that a great deal of what she believed would depend on how the 'eye-witness' accounts were passed on. He didn't know what had been repeated about him. One thing was sure, he didn't dare go rushing back to his ranch, for they would certainly be looking for him there. His best chance was to stick to the mountains, living off the land as long as he could stand the hard diet. Perhaps he could get some salt and a shotgun from the ranch some night, if they had left the place alone.

★   ★   ★

Bart Dodge was happier than he had been in months. He could feel a lightness that seemed to forecast an end to his financial problems. He felt that he was as clean as a hound's tooth, so far as the disappearance of the stallion was concerned. He had been in the sheriff's office with Bristol himself when the disturbance with Parker had occurred at the dance. And neither he nor any of his men had ridden in pursuit of Walker.

Sam Parker was dead and could tell no tales, and it looked as if his death had made Walker a wanted murderer. He smiled when he thought about it, for in killing Parker he had thought merely to silence him; he hadn't envisioned the happy coincidence that made it appear that Walker had killed the man. Bart was anxious to talk to Lash Wade who was busy hiding the stallion. Now as the setting sun lingered on the tips of the Purples, he glimpsed his ramrod riding toward the ranch. Bart got an expensive cigar from the box on his desk, clipped the end and strode back to the window. Wade was hitching the horse to the rack outside, not bothering to unsaddle. The foreman waved to an idle hand angling across the yard and the man came to take the horse.

Bart lighted up the cigar as Lash came through the door. As the foreman smiled at him, Bart suddenly resented him. Lash knew that Bart was dependent on him, and after last night he was more dependent than ever. Now Dodge imagined that there was hint of this knowledge in Wade's smug smile, and he frowned.

'Well?' asked Bart. He detested the way everything had to be dragged out of Wade, and then the way Wade would give every boring detail before coming out with the main facts.

'Well what, boss?' asked Wade dropping exhausted into an upholstered chair.

'Why, you know damn well what! What about the horse?'

'Oh, the hoss,' grinned Lash. He indicated with his smile that there was a lot to tell about the horse and that he would get to it in his own way.

'Yes, the horse. Now stop grinning and tell what happened.'

'Nothing happened,' laughed Wade, still not revealing anything. 'Everything went accordin' to plan. We led the hoss away durin' the fight and put him in a stall at the livery stable. We took him out about five this mawnin' after Carl got old Holt drunk. We brought him up the valley and didn't see a soul.'

Dodge was nervous; this was only part of the story. He waited agonizing seconds before he said: 'How about the paint?'

Wade laughed. 'Well, we got him painted, an' what a job that was. First we got three or four ropes on him, but once he smelled that paint he went plumb wild an' we musta put a dozen more ropes around him. We finally dropped him down on his side and painted that side first. Then he rolled over and got dirt and

136

dust in all of the paint. We had to move in close and untangle him so he could stand up but when we dropped him again he went right down on the same side and we had to do it all ag'in. We got him the next time, though—that green kid we put on—he got his arm busted in the tussle. Bud got a whole can of paint dumped on his outfit and he's mad as a hornet, but that horse is the blackest stallion we got right now and he's in the horse herd where nobody'd ever think of looking for him. As long as it don't rain an' wash off that water paint, he's a black for a spell!'

Dodge looked out at the sun-scorched grass. 'I won't mind if it does rain. We can always paint the horse again.'

'Did you hear about Walker?' asked Wade.

Dodge whirled around, sensing that Wade knew something special and deliberately had held it back.

'You've some news about Walker? Why didn't you come right out with it?'

'I thought maybe you knew.' Wade was smiling slightly.

'Out with it, then. Do you have to beat around the bush with everything, Lash?'

'I'm not beating around any bush, boss. All I know is that we saw Wally Bristol comin' down the valley with some of the boys from town an' we rode over to see how they made out. Walker got clean away.'

Dodge sank into a chair. All day he had been hoping for a different report. He had wished for swift, harsh, rope-justice, or to hear that Bristol had chased the small rancher out of the county. Even taking him back for a trial would have been something. He didn't think it possible that Walker, on a borrowed horse, could elude the posse.

'How could he get away?' Bart queried.

'He picked a danged good hoss for one thing. You know he got Ed Weaver's big bay, the one they call Happy, and he led them up the valley all night long at an easy gallop. Killed six horses with that damn easy gallop, that Happy did. Another twenty riders quit after fifteen miles.'

'But there were more men than that. How could he outrun so many?' Dodge crushed his cigar and threw it on the rug.

Lash felt new importance and he leaned forward. 'Then he hit for the mountains—made a beeline for Glass Mountain!'

'Why, I've hunted those trails—and Almstock Creek cuts a canyon through there that no man can cross,' declared Dodge, his expression incredulous.

'That's right. They all thought they had Walker when he did a fool thing like heading straight for Glass Mountain, but they figured he was new around here and didn't know what he was doing. You see, they didn't figure that he was gonna pull this stunt at the bridge.' Lash

138

began to roll a cigarette.

'Bridge? What bridge? There's no bridge over the canyon, except—'

'Except that rotted old thing about two miles up,' interrupted Wade. 'Walker took the hoss across that old bridge—rode him across, mind you. They all saw it happen and held their breath. They said the hoss picked his way over the bridge, and at the last minute when both back legs went through the rotten boards, Walker slid off and pulled the hoss through.'

'They saw all this and didn't shoot? What the devil was the matter with them?'

'Why, to hear them tell it you could see that they was concentrating all their minds on whether or not Walker would make it. They just couldn't shoot at a man taking a chance like that. The canyon's a hundred feet deep at that point. You wouldn't shoot at a poor fool buckin' odds like that, would you, boss?'

'If I'd been there, he'd never have made it,' declared Dodge.

'I still don't see how he could do it. I was up there last year an' that bridge was rotten as hell. This Walker's awful lucky at times, ain't he, boss?'

'His luck has run out. Just because he crossed a rotten bridge is no sign he's goin' to get the better of me. Did Wally say what he's gonna do? Is he gonna go after Walker?'

Lash shook his head. 'No. He said he was

gonna sleep a couple of days before he did anything. They were a beat bunch of fellas that come down out of the Purples, an' those hosses was knocked out some, too.'

Dodge strode to the window and looked out, then he cut back to the center of the room. He got a fresh cigar from the desk and then as an afterthought brought the box to Lash and offered the foreman one. They both puffed deeply and savored the smoke. Wade was happy as he could be from the expression on his face. Dodge, too, seemed to be delighted.

'You know, Lash,' the rancher said, 'for awhile I was sorry that Walker didn't get it last night, but now I'm kind of glad he's still around. For one thing, people will start to consider him a nuisance after last night. For another thing, we can use a scapegoat now—if we could hang just one more thing on him.'

'What you got in mind now?' laughed the foreman.

'This isn't something new,' admitted Bart. 'All along I've known we needed a shot in the arm for this place and I knew the first place I'd try when the time came.' Dodge smiled and said no more.

'What kind of a shot in the arm?' asked Wade sharply. The foreman's expression indicated that he surmised his job was in some way in jeopardy.

'Why, cash-money. Cash, of course—what

else is there to boost up a sagging business? Nice fresh cash, and lots of it.' Dodge threw back his head and laughed.

'Where in the hell are you gonna lay your hands on any cash?' asked Wade, his tone relieved.

'Why, I'll go back to the bank, of course,' said Dodge.

'You'll go to the bank, eh?' chuckled Lash. Then, correctly reading Bart Dodge's implication, he frowned. 'You ain't serious? The bank in Purple? You mean we'll rob the bank? Gawd, that's risky. How in hell do you expect to get away with a thing like that? You mean stay right here in the valley afterward, livin' with all the people you robbed of their life savin's?'

'That's the best way. This bank is a cinch—and don't look so scared. Where do you think I got the money to buy this place? Oh, don't worry, I always worked in between, because you don't have to worry about spending money if you work, but watch out if you don't work and then start spending it.'

'Why, it's loco! You'll never get away with a thing like this. They'll have us like nothing. Listen, now don't look at me like I was yellow. I got the guts for somethin' like this and so have a few of the boys, but for Gawd's sake let's hit the bank and run. Live here afterward? Hell no, I ain't that kind. Why, it gives me the

141

willies just to think of tryin' to be friends with somebody I robbed.'

Dodge shook his head. 'I've got a fortune invested right here and if it ever rains and the springs come back, we can run five thousand head a year to market. I'm not leavin' what I got and I'm not losin' it, either, and a little cash is all we need to tide us over until winter. But why bother with a little when we can make a big haul, and then blame it on Jim Walker?'

Wade gasped, open-mouthed. 'How in hell can we do that? Last night was a freak with him blunderin' along just as we silenced Parker. Now, how can we blame the bank robbery on him? And while you're at it, you better tell me how we get in the safe at the bank?'

'We can use the horse to frame him. I haven't figured the details yet,' began Dodge, 'but it can be done. We have the horse now, and with him painted black he shouldn't be too hard to keep hidden. When the time comes I'll have the horse to help put the blame on Walker. Maybe we could use the horse on the job and then leave him up at Walker's place in the corral. Anybody that saw that horse near the bank wouldn't forget him too easy. As far as the bank safe goes, I know a gent in Wyoming that can blow it for a price. I want you to go to Brown's Hole, Wyoming. You ever been there?'

Wade stood up. 'I been in Wyoming plenty, of course, but I ain't never been to Brown's

142

Hole. What's the name of this fella you want me to talk to?'

CHAPTER FIFTEEN

Jim Walker stuck to the hills for a few days but the lure of the valley and what was happening to his ranch and things at the cabin finally brought him to quitting the wild country. It was late afternoon when he headed out of the mountain brakes. His plan was to travel through the valley in the darkness and visit the Ackerman place. He counted on the fact that they would still be friendly to him, although he was uncertain of the feelings of Sally after the events of the dance. From them he hoped to learn the condition of his stock and whether his own place was being watched—either by Wally Bristol or Dodge's men.

Jim couldn't understand why anybody that had as much of this world's goods as Dodge had would worry about someone like himself, and yet he could see the jealousy in the other's eyes whenever they met face to face. He also wanted to find out from Dan Ackerman if the silver stallion had turned up anywhere in the valley. If anyone had learned anything it would be Sally's voluble father. Thinking back, everything was confusing. The fight with Sam Parker had seemed almost planned and he was sure that Dodge had a hand in it. The murder of the ruffian was inexplicable. How could they have ever planned anything to come off as closely as that incident?

He didn't have the slightest idea who had shot the big man. He'd had only a fleeting glimpse of the slight form of the murderer. He decided that they could not possibly have planned to frame him for the murder of Sam Parker. His running hadn't helped his own case, but considering the large crowd at the dance, he figured he had used reasonably good judgment. The important thing was that the murder of Parker was an unfortunate coincidence with his appearance on the scene, and he doubted that anyone would believe his story. Parker had been killed for some other reason, but what could it be? If Dodge had brought him to the dance to raise trouble he surely had no reason to silence Parker's story, for no one could prove it was authentic or not. He considered that Dodge might have done the killing to keep from paying Parker for his part in the fight. Yet Dodge was apparently wealthy, open-handed enough, and surely he wouldn't go so far as to kill the man to avoid paying him or to close his mouth. Dodge had plenty of money and didn't need to kill a false witness.

In the past few days, Jim Walker had had a thousand thoughts about the remarks that

Wade and Dodge had made to Sheriff Bristol that day in front of the Ackerman ranch after Jim had killed Neal Spaker. They knew something of Jim's past, that much was sure. And even Wally Bristol had believed them enough to check if Walker was a member of the notorious Wild Bunch.

He wondered if Bristol had really done any investigating or if the lawman had just let the remark drop at the dance to throw a scare into him. Bristol seemed to like him and he hoped the lawman would give him a break. The days in Star Valley and Brown's Hole and in the Old Outlaw Trail country of Wyoming, from Robber's Roost to The Hole-in-the-Wall, were behind him. He wished they would stay there; even Butch Cassidy was said to have left the country. The bunch was busted and broken and peace had come to Wyoming. The Johnson County War was over and the outlaws it had made had come and gone. With them went Walker, an orphan of the fight. If he was lightning fast with a gun it was not all his fault. He didn't care if he ever wore a weapon again as long as he lived. He had felt the butt of his Colt slam against his palm once too often already, and many a night was haunted by the faces of the victims of his gun.

Then where did Dodge find out about his past? Dodge must have known him or seen him when he was riding with Butch Cassidy.

Cassidy was famous and pointed to by one and all; therefore it was possible that Dodge had seen him with Butch.

As he rode along the high trail, something made him glance downward and he drew in the bay, watching with interest the rider on the trail below him. The lower trail paralleled the upper one that he followed, except that where his trail merely led from the wild country around Glass Mountain to Purple Valley, the lower trail ran through the mountain pass over into Wyoming. Jim had no difficulty in recognizing the rider as Lash Wade, both from his black and white pinto and the peculiar habitual weaving of his body in the saddle. But it seemed strange that Wade would be riding alone down the trail from Wyoming. As a rule, he knew that Wade had a couple of Pitchfork riders with him. Curious, Jim spurred the bay to a gallop.

At the sound of Jim's running horse above him, Jim saw Wade turn in his saddle and look up. Then he swung back, spurring the pinto hard. Leaning over like a jockey, the Pitchfork foreman laid the quirt against the pinto's flanks and the horse ran his best.

The race was odd, for interception was impossible for hours at the soonest. The higher ground that Walker rode was separated from the lower parallel trail by a steep bank of sharply outcropped rock, which was impossible to descend and equally impossible to climb up.

All the two men could do was to ride along within sight of each other for miles, each hoping to be the first to reach the point, miles ahead, where the two trails met, and thereby gain some advantage. For Wade, who seemed to be riding for his life, the advantage would be to get a long start on Walker at the trail crossing, then hope to make it to the nearest Pitchfork line shack.

To Walker the object of the race was to be waiting for Wade where the trails met, and he knew he would have to ride the bay hard over a rocky trail to do it. Temporarily Wade was pulling ahead. Jim's advantage was that he could shoot at the other quite easily, whereas Wade would have to keep turning and firing at someone a hundred yards above his head from the back of a bobbing horse. Wade didn't even draw his gun.

Walker, however, fired every now and then just to keep Wade pinned closer to the rock wall where he couldn't travel at any great speed. Every shot brought a frightened backward glance from Wade and a slower pace as he reined the pinto against the sharp incline. Jim came to a sharp declivity that led into a draw dangerously filled with large round boulders. He skirted it, running back from the rim at an angle, and lost valuable time getting around it.

When he once more came back to the edge of the higher ground he caught a glimpse of Wade far ahead and going like the wind. Wade had gained so much ground that he doubted if he could catch him at the meeting of the trails. His own path now led away from the rim, and every foot of the way he would be letting Wade get a little farther ahead.

One fantastic chance was still left. Jim could ride straight ahead and swerve sharply in an attempt to take the horse down the almost sheer slippery rock that divided the two trails. Wade had to swing wide at this point and follow a wide jug-handle curve, and by riding straight ahead, Jim could intercept Lash Wade's trail. Then if he could make the perilous descent safely he could cut the other off.

Without thinking twice, Jim decided to risk the slim chance, and drove the bay horse forward. The rim was three hundred yards off; the distance quickly shrank to a hundred. He had lost sight of Lash when he had swung away from the rim, and he could only guess his approximate location.

Jim reined up at the edge. Now he could see Wade, still far back up the trail and riding as if chased by the very devil. Wade glanced up and saw him sitting on the bay at the edge of the cliff. He looked again as if to make sure he had not seen an apparition. And he slashed madly at the foam-flecked flanks of the pinto.

Jim looked up and down the bank trying to find the easiest descent. The angle was frightening and there was no foothold for the horse, just smooth shale stretching down with small vertical seams running parallel to any course down the decline. If it had been a dirt cutbank or even sand, Walker would have thought nothing of it, but smooth hard rock . . . Surely the horse would fall and start to roll, and once that happened he was lost. He heard Wade cry out, calling for more speed from the pinto, no doubt suspecting what was in Jim's mind.

Walker put the spur to the horse as there was no better place than where they now stood. The animal quivered for a moment; Walker jabbed with his heels again and the bay placed first one forefoot and then the other over the edge and neighed with fear as the abrupt downward slide began. Below and coming at a gallop, Wade opened fire and Jim heard the bullets whining off the rock surfaces around himself and the horse. The rear feet of the bay went over the top with a clumsy pitch and the animal lurched away at frightening speed, struggling frantically for balance.

They slipped and slid with the iron horseshoes throwing sparks across the hard rock surface. Now the animal lifted one foot and drove to the side in a desperate maneuver that narrowly avoided a jagged rock. The horse's hind feet slid under him and for an instant he was sitting down and still sliding but he came up off the rock and continued to skid. Walker felt a bullet tug at his sleeve, and then they struck the lower trail, the horse stumbling and throwing Jim over its head.

He sailed through the air with an involuntary cry of alarm but managed to land like a cat on all fours and come staggering up with his bare Colt in his hand.

The bay struggled frantically to his feet and blocked the trail so that Wade, cursing, had to rein in. The foreman sat still; the pinto was blowing badly and spraddle-legged from the tough run. Wade's gun was empty, and as he looked into the barrel of Walker's Colt he made no move. He was beaten by Walker's fantastic slide down the rock and Wade had no notion of going against a man who had the nerve and daring to attempt it.

'You're a fool, Walker, to try a stunt like that—you mighta killed that hoss!' he declared. 'How come you're chasin' me, anyhow?'

Jim smiled. 'Climb down, Lash, and we'll talk about why I chased you.'

'No. You got no reason to hold me up. Stand aside, Walker; you're in enough trouble already without gettin' in deeper!'

'Where's the stallion, Lash?'

'What stallion?' Wade raised his eyebrows.

Walker laughed. 'Oh, come off it, Wade; don't be silly. I've got you clean and I can make you talk easy enough, so why put yourself through that just for Bart Dodge? I know you fellas pinched the stallion while I was fighting with Sam Parker and I've a hunch that your gang had something to do with Parker's killin', too. But first, what did you do with Silver Cloud?'

'You ain't gettin' nothin' from me, Walker,' Wade sneered.

'Oh, I'll get it, all right, Lash. Climb on down, an' hurry up!'

Wade stepped out of the saddle and stood awkwardly waiting.

'Just catch up your bridle, Lash. We'll lead these broncs down the trail a ways.' Walker caught up the reins of the bay and motioned the Pitchfork foreman to go ahead of him.

CHAPTER SIXTEEN

They walked the horses down the trail with Lash constantly staring back at Jim. A half-hour later found them in a wooded area and Jim hitched the animals to a serviceberry shrub. Taking the rope from the saddle, he turned to Wade.

'Sit down, Lash, and put your hands behind that sapling.'

Wade got down sullenly and put his hands behind him. Jim drew the rope up tight around his wrists and he heard the Pitchfork foreman

151

suck in his breath in pain. With Wade helpless, Jim came around in front of him and squatted down. He began to build a cigarette.

'Gimme a smoke will you, Walker?' entreated Wade.

'You better not smoke, Lash. Smoke can hurt a body.'

'Yeah, sure—but how about a smoke, Walker, old pal?'

'Where's the horse, Lash?'

'You'll never get me to open my mouth, Walker.'

'Where you been? Where were you coming from?'

Wade blinked. He wasn't expecting any questions on where he'd been. 'None o' yore business!'

'It sure must be my business, if you're afraid to tell me,' Walker declared. He quickly added, 'Wyoming is where you been—any fool can tell that. But what were you doing there that you're scared stiff I'll find out about? I wonder what's so important to make your face go wild like that.'

'My face ain't goin' wild. Go ahead and beat me up if you think you can make me talk. I don't care if you kick my brains out.'

'I got somethin' better than that in mind,' Jim said grimly.

'You're lyin'. You're tryin' to scare me, is all.'

152

'We'll see about that, old timer. Sit still there and rest your back against the tree while I go break some wood. Slack your backbone and relax a little, Lash—while you can.'

Walker turned his back and started breaking dry branches over his knee. He built up a sizeable pile of firewood before he stopped and kindled some twigs. He sat down and piled on the branches, starting with the twigs and building slowly so that he soon had a crackling blaze. Flames leaped and danced before the fascinated eyes of Wade who had to draw in his boots to keep them from the fire.

'Where's the horse, Lash?'

'Go to hell.'

'You did steal the horse, though.'

'Of course, we stole the critter, you fool. It was easy enough, but you'll never see him again.' Wade started to laugh.

Jim reached forward and passed a few turns of the rope around Wade's feet and jerked them forward. Then going back, he passed the rope through the fork of a nearby sapling. He hoisted the feet of the struggling Wade into the air and held them above the fire while flame tips licked at the foreman's bootheels.

Sweat stood out on Wade's brow. 'You're crazy, Walker!'

'Maybe,' said Walker.

'Let me go—an' I won't tell anybody about this,' said Wade, suddenly begging.

'I'll let the rope off some to take some of the tension off your legs, Lash. But of course, your feet'll be a little closer to the fire. There—how's that?'

'Ouch!' yelled Wade, grimacing with pain.

'Hot, eh, Lash? How about the horse? Maybe you never see a gent get burned this way before, eh? Feel those hamstring cords getting hot in the back o' your legs? Funny thing, a guy can't walk without those muscles. Can't even keep your balance without them. Don't take much of a fire to ruin them for life.'

'Owww! Oh—please, Walker, for Gawd's sake, pull up on the rope!' screamed Wade, twisting and trying to hold his legs higher in the air.

'Where's the horse?'

'Okay, okay—I'll tell. The horse is with our herd. It's painted like a black.'

'Painted?'

'Yes—the rope, for Gawd's sake—pull up on the rope. I can't hold my feet out of the fire any longer. You promised!'

Walker lowered his feet a little toward the fire. Wade screamed in pain.

'Why'd you go over to Wyoming?'

'Ouch! Ow, oh, oh! To get Mold Dillon from Brown's Hole. To get Dillon. Pull up on the rope. Pull up the rope!'

'Dillon?' Walker pulled the feet to safety. 'Dillon, the safe cracker?'

'Yes. Oh, Gawd, I talked, didn't I?'

Jim lowered the feet once more and asked, 'Why does Dodge want Dillon?'

'Ouch! He's gonna rob the bank and blame you for the job; use your—ouch!—use your hoss to frame you. Pull up—pull up. Walker, my feet are killing me.'

Walker pulled the feet high above the fire.

'Wade, now I'm gonna talk. You listen close to what I say. I'm gonna drop your feet right into that fire.'

'No! No, please,' begged Wade.

'Then if I let you go you hit out of this country—back over the mountains the way you came and don't ever come back here. Do you understand? You don't say anything to anybody. You just ride the fastest you can.'

Wade couldn't believe his good fortune. 'You mean you're really gonna let me go, Walker? You're gonna let me light a shuck?'

Walker nodded. 'That's right, Lash, I'm lettin' you go—free and clear.'

'By Gawd, Walker, you're pure steel. I'll never forget this, or you. Jim, I'll ride straight as an arrow and I won't stop till I come to where they never heard of Jim Walker.'

'You do that, Wade, you ride along. Sorry I can't do anything for your legs.'

'Oh, don't worry about that. Listen, Walker, I'm gonna do one more thing for you before I ride on. You been square as a corner with me. I

155

guess I don't have to tell you this but I'm goin' to because I hate to see them hang anything on a regular guy like you. I'd be dead now if Dodge had me like you did!'

Walker raised his eyebrows. 'What's this about, Lash?'

'Craig Briggs is the gent that plugged Parker, Jim!'

A wave of relief swept over Walker. He hadn't thought his kindness in letting Wade go would ever result in a windfall of information like this.

'Craig Briggs?'

'Yeah, he's a sneak with a gun. Watch out for him, Jim, he was always tryin' to get my job at Pitchfork. I wouldn't do the job for Dodge, but Briggs jumped at the chance.'

'But why kill the man? I don't see why Dodge should have had him shot.'

'Dodge got him over here from Star Valley to fake the thing about the horse. It was just a diversion to get you into a fight and make the ownership of the horse cloudier still. He promised Parker three hundred dollars for provoking the fight and claiming the horse was his. Then Dodge established his own alibi by having one of the boys get thrown in the jug just before the fight started. That way, he was with Wally Bristol all the time. I got Cloud when the crowd gathered and slipped him off to the livery stable. We hid him in a box stall until near morning.'

'But they killed Parker—'

'Listen, Walker, there's one thing you and everybody else can't get through their heads. Dodge is near busted and three hundred is like three thousand to him right now—it's that sweet. Everything he does is a big front. That's one reason he wants that horse so bad; it would bring a thousand dollars of anybody's money. Don't be fooled by all the riders he keeps around. The water situation has got him licked, and a few more months will bust him for sure. Why, if Morton and the other guys he owes all jumped at once, they'd take his hide.'

'That's why he's going to rob the bank, eh, Lash?'

'That's the whole thing. He's robbed banks before, I guess, so he'll probably bring it off this time. He's gonna use the stallion to pin the job on you, Jim.'

'That may not be easy,' said Walker grimly. He untied Lash Wade's hands and watched the foreman painfully limp to his horse. Jim helped the foreman to mount and he stood holding the cheek-piece of the pinto's bridle and looking up at the man.

'Funny thing, Walker,' Wade said, 'us being on opposite sides. I always hated you but now that I see what a straight shooter you are, I wish I was stayin' on here as your friend. I really like you.'

'Here's your gun, Wade. You're kind of a good guy, yourself. When you get across the mountains and get settled down, steer clear of anybody like Dodge.' Jim smiled.

'By Gawd, don't hand me that pistol butt-first like that, Jim, it's too much.' The voice of the foreman broke. 'Don't worry, I won't try to shoot you and I won't come back along your trail, either. So long, pal!' Wade started up toward the mountains, again turning and waving as he went. Several times he turned and shouted goodbye before he was out of sight.

Walker stood smiling. The gun hadn't been loaded, and he hoped Wade would check it soon, in case he needed it in the lonely trip through the mountain pass. He turned and mounted the bay. They were just above the valley floor and night was coming swiftly as the mountains threw their shadows across Purple Valley.

He rode for the Ackerman spread in light spirits, looking forward to seeing Sally and old Dan Ackerman once more.

*   *   *

The lights were shining from the windows of the Ackerman place when he finally rode into the yard. Walker was relieved because he knew it to be at least ten o'clock, and from previous experience he knew that they generally retired

158

early. However, on this night at least, they had company. A tall black stallion stood hitched outside the high corral fence. The bay whickered excitedly at the black horse but Walker attached no significance to this greeting. He tied his own horse behind the house and walked quietly to the front door. He could hear voices inside. He knocked once and thrust open the door.

Sally Ackerman let out a shriek at the sudden intrusion. There were two men in the room; one was old Ackerman and the other was Weaver, who owned the Window Sash spread down the valley. Old Ackerman's jaw dropped at the wild-looking figure in the doorway. Walker hadn't judged beforehand the effect of his appearance suddenly thrust upon others. His week's growth of beard twisted on his face, pitch black and thick as a hound's fur. His light-blue eyes caught the light of the kerosene lamps and for a moment they flickered wildly throwing back the yellow light in blank reflection. His clothes, always patched and threadbare when he was leading a normal life, were now in scarecrow condition.

Long grass was caught here and there in his garments and clusters of burrs clung to him. One sleeve had been ripped off above the elbow and his hard bicep shimmered in the lamplight.

'Why, you dirty hoss thief!' was Weaver's opening greeting. He kicked over his chair and

159

came to his feet with a pistol in his hand. The movement of Weaver was greased lightning; he was a hard-bitten scrapper in spite of his fifty-odd years. His roar could cow the timid but in spite of his fast movement he was beaten clean by Walker whose pistol was drawn and cocked before Weaver's gun had cleared leather.

Weaver blinked, looking at the Colt in Jim Walker's hand.

'Better put away your iron, Mr Weaver, 'cause your horse is hitched out in back. He's fat in the belly with the heavy grass from the high meadows around Glass Mountain. He's fit as a fiddle except he might need a new pair of shoes. I think we scraped some iron off in a little brush I had this afternoon.'

Weaver's expression softened. 'My bay horse is all right! Did you hear that?' He looked at the others with a foolish expression, his pistol barrel tipped floorward. 'The bay is out back—Happy's out back!'

'I got ears, you old fool, I just been sitting here tellin' you no harm would come to the hoss. I been tellin' you for the last two hours that Walker is as fast as a comet's tail. So you jump up like a damn kid and try to pull a gun on him. Walker's got a hair-trigger brain or he'd of blasted you to hell with one curl of his finger,' declared Old Ackerman.

'I—I'm sorry, Walker. You sure had me

160

packed meat!' admitted Weaver.

'I'm sorry I had to take your horse, Mr Weaver, but he was the best I could find in ten seconds,' said Jim, and he looked at Sally.

'He's the best you could find in ten years, you young whippersnapper,' said Weaver, ''cept maybe Silver Cloud. Nothing can touch that hoss. When I see you had my hoss, I reared back and called for bets. I wouldn't bust my rump runnin' after Happy because I knew he'd show his tail to the rest of the boneshakers in this county. Why, I cleaned up a fortune in bets an' I could buy three more horses like Happy, but there'd still be just one Happy to me. I'll always love a bay horse because o' him! I just gotta go out and look him over. I'll be back in a minute.'

Walker and Sally were staring at one another.

Old Ackerman cleared his throat and glanced at the young couple.

'I gotta see that bay myself,' he murmured and he followed Weaver outside. The door closed.

Sally allowed herself to smile; her expression had been one of deep concern for him. He smiled back at her.

'I guess I'm a mess, eh, Sally? I sure hated to miss takin' you home from the dance the other night. Did you get home all right?'

'Jim Walker, is that all you're worried about—that I got home all right? Don't you

161

know there's a reward on your head? Don't you know that they think you killed Sam Parker in Purple? Oh, Jim, you poor dear!'

She burst out crying and ran into his arms. Walker stood awkwardly, not knowing what to do. He put his arm on her back. She looked up at him, crying softly, the tears running from her eyes. Walker was lost for words and he tentatively dabbed with his forefinger at one of the tears on her softly curved cheek.

'I better not touch you till I'm washed—that is, if you want me to touch you again,' he stammered.

She tipped up her face and kissed him and his face grew hot while sweat broke out on his forehead. She kissed him again and he felt his knees begin to turn to jelly.

She stepped back, laughing. 'Why, you're weak, Jim! One or two kisses and you're as weak as a new-born calf. Look at your legs shake.'

'I'm a little hungry,' he admitted touching his stomach. 'Funny thing is that it didn't bother me much till you started kissin' me, Sally. You got a bite to eat for a guy that ain't ate much but a few scrawny birds and a couple of rabbits this week?'

'Oh, heaven forgive me, Jim! For golly sakes', sit down at the table while I rustle up some food for you. Whatever in the world is the matter with me? I'm a fool.'

Jim sat at the table and smiled weakly as she flew about the room getting a meal ready for him.

CHAPTER SEVENTEEN

After he had eaten and adjusted his tight belt and eaten still more of Sally's wonderful cooking, they sat and talked. The Ackermans and Weaver told Jim how his place had been burned to the ground by Dodge's riders one night, and how some of his stock had disappeared the following night. He listened grimly as they told of Craig Briggs and the way the little Pitchfork rider was bragging about burning his ranch buildings. Ackerman had run what was left of Jim's stock in with his own stuff so that Pitchfork wouldn't be able to get it all. Wally Bristol had posted a reward for his capture—it wasn't much, just a hundred dollars, the standard amount that the county kept in escrow for murderers. However, it was a bounty and it was thought that a Pitchfork rider might try and collect it if the opportunity came.

'Mister Weaver,' began Walker, 'outside, hitched to the corral, you got a fine big black that I'd like to ride for a few days if you could see your way—'

'Take him! Take him, Jim. His name is Tar Bucket! As long as I got Happy, that's all I care about. Say, I can just see the look on my youngsters' faces when I fork that Happy into the barn. I'll say, "Well, here's old Happy back—I just rode up to Glass Mountain where that mean ole outlaw Jim Walker lives! I just rode up there, an' I says: 'Hey Jim, you look like a tolerable good cuss to me. How about tradin' hosses, now that you gave the law the slip?'"' He looked around at the amused faces at the table. 'Do you mind if I put it that way, Jim?'

Jim laughed.

'That's all right with me, Mr Weaver.' He broke off without telling them the rest of his plan.

Weaver left soon after that and Walker promised to return the black horse soon. Old Ackerman turned in early and Sally and Jim went outside while Jim adjusted the stirrups and set up the cinches on the big black horse. Finally, though he took five times as long as the job required, he was finished and he turned slowly to the girl with the reins of the black in his hand.

'Well, Sally, I guess it's so long for a while longer.'

'What will you do, Jim?' she asked, coming close and playing with the neck-string on his battered hat.

'I'll try to see Bristol and clear myself of the murder charge—you see, I know who did it, but I didn't want to say anything in front of your dad or Weaver. Craig Briggs did the killing, but I don't want word to get out that I know about it, or he'd leave the valley before I could pin it on him. I know where Silver Cloud is, too, and the first thing I'm going to do is get a hold of him!'

'Jim you'll be killed! Why don't you leave the valley? Run for it while there's still a chance; there's too much against you. Dodge has everything going for him!'

'Well, he's had a good time up till now, but he made one mistake, Sally.'

She looked up at him. 'What mistake, Jim?'

'He burned my place. He burned down my place, an' I built it and owned it free and clear.'

Sally looked up into the pale blue eyes and now they had caught the silver moonlight and were blankly reflecting it, as they had done with the lamplight in the cabin. She shuddered and fell against his chest.

'Don't look like that, Jim. Don't get that look in your eyes. It was the same the day you went for Neal Spaker—I saw it in your eyes that day, too. Darling, run from the valley. You'll be killed, you haven't a chance!'

'I'll see you soon,' he promised and kissed her lightly. Tar Bucket spun around as Walker put his toe in the stirrup. Walker went hopping with the horse and swung gracefully into the saddle. He looked down at the tear-stained cheeks of the girl. He touched his hat in a farewell salute and rode the horse out of the yard. Sobbing, the girl ran to the house.

Walker headed for the Pitchfork ranch where the horse herd was pulled in close, due to the water situation. He slowed up when he got near the stock and edged cautiously closer to see if there were any night guards with the herd. He saw none. He walked the black horse in closer to the horse herd until he was on the fringe of it. Then he saw one head above the others, one set of wild eyes shining brighter than all the others, one horse stepping briskly through the nervous herd, ears pricked up sharply at the sounds of the rider.

The stallion whickered joyfully and Walker was sure the black he looked at was Silver Cloud, still here in the herd and recognizing his scent. Walker reached down and shook out a few coils of rope. He moved Tar Bucket into the nervous pack that was starting to run slowly. He kept his eye on the horse and whirled the rope slowly, dropped a loop over the horse's head and stopped the black.

Silver Cloud did not fight the rope. Instead, he stopped instantly as the rest of the horses loped by slowly. Jim dropped from the saddle, went to the animal, and quickly gave him sugar that he had brought from the Ackermans'.

Walker wet his finger and rubbed it on the horse's back; in the moonlight he could see the stain of the water paint on his finger. Jim shifted the saddle from Tar Bucket to Silver Cloud, then he whipped the black horse into the herd. He had no time to lose, there were still other things to do this night.

Now he rode for the Dodge ranch, keeping alert for any signs of night guards among the cattle that surrounded the place. There were no riders around, apparently because the cattle were bunched so close to the ranch itself. The Pitchfork hands could spring from their bunks and go into instant action. Walker kept this in mind as he rode toward the buildings. He had to be careful; it would be foolish to get caught by these men, and he knew he could count on no justice at their hands.

He could smell the stacked hay, three huge piles of it. They were probably the biggest haystacks in the valley, as Dodge went in for bigness in everything, whether there was profit in it or not. He could see the outlines of the mounds against the sky as he came closer. The hay represented all the first cutting for the Pitchfork spread and with what he had, Dodge could at least insure that his herd would not run out of graze for the next month or so; the hay might even tide the rancher over till rain came.

Walker dropped silently from the saddle at the first pile. Leading Silver Cloud, he quickly ran to the side that was away from the ranch house and other buildings. He struck a match and watched with expressionless eyes as the flame ate down one strand of the tinder-dry grass and then caught on another and so on until a patch the size of a bushel was burning.

Silver Cloud whickered excitedly as Jim jumped back into the saddle and rode quickly to the next pile of hay; once more he dropped from the saddle. Now behind him he heard the fire whoosh through the pile taking it beyond saving in one gigantic skyward leap of flame. Almost in the same instant a voice cried, 'Fire!'

He was in the saddle again and riding hard for the third pile of hay. A shot rang out and he heard the whine of a bullet overhead. He dropped down next to the stack and fumbled with a match; it went out. Behind him he could hear a second shout.

'The hay! The hay's on fire!'

Another voice shouted, 'Turn out, turn out! All hands, turn out! Come on, you sleepy fools, the hay's on fire. Get the ones that did it!'

Walker thought he recognized Dodge's voice. He struck a second match and this one caught a slender strand of hay; the stack roared upward, the long yellow tongue creeping through the pile and seeking the highest point. As he mounted the stallion, men were running out of the bunkhouse, cursing and hollering. It was as light as day and Walker quickly rode into the shadows. He turned in the saddle to see if there would be any pursuit. At least, he now had the fastest horse in the valley to give them a good run for it.

But pursuit was not being organized. Great blazing swatches from the roaring stacks were lifting skyward by the invisible waves of the three fires' drafts, and these were coming down everywhere. Ladders were raised to the buildings' roofs and Dodge himself could be seen up on top, stomping out the burning patches of hay wherever they fell. Walker rode farther away and turned to watch once more; the men looked like toys running about in the flickering light of the fires. Jim sat his horse, fascinated by the wildness of the scene.

Every available bucket was in service and the water was quickly passed to the point where it was most needed. A great deal of it was sloshed or wasted as the men, excited by the three leaping fires which were roaring so loudly that hearing was impossible, fell and stumbled as they sloshed the water ineffectively. Now one of the lesser sheds roared into life, a mixture of bright orange, black smoke and fiery sparks as the bone-dry timber went flaming skyward.

To the south Walker could see the horse herd running pell-mell, and now another unforeseen event began to take place. The cattle had begun to move and they came pounding toward the ranch but the sight of the fire turned them as they approached the first stack. They swept around it and into the ranchyard, and the firefighters ran for their lives. The roof of the ranch house was the roosting place of most of the men, who watched, paralyzed with fear, as the stampeding cows swept through. The bunkhouse went next and as the cows passed by the men dropped from the ranch house roof and ran to attempt to save the lesser structure.

Somehow the flames were coming from the inside and the men halted with shouts of dismay before the bright-windowed building. They didn't try to save it; they watched as their belongings disappeared in the blaze. The first stack was gone now and only a low fiery ball of glowing red remained.

Walker headed for the town of Purple. He hoped no one had been hurt in the blaze, although his concern didn't go so far as to include Dodge himself or the diminutive Craig Briggs.

He remembered the slight form the night of Parker's killing, and while he had not recognized him at that time he now associated the figure he had seen with that of Briggs. He heard fresh shouting and cursing behind him. Looking back, he saw that the ranch house was partially in flames, the frantic forms of the men casting huge, grotesque shadows along the valley floor as they fought the fire. All the stacks were reduced to small, glowing heaps and

Walker smiled grimly, thinking that he had paid Dodge back for burning him out; now he wanted to tend to another detail. He swung the stallion into a gallop and felt the fresh wind blowing against his bearded face; he wondered if most people would recognize him with the heavy beard and riding on the painted horse. It was unlikely at night, he thought, so to make better time, he stuck to the valley road.

CHAPTER EIGHTEEN

Sheriff Wally Bristol liked to sit up late. In fact, after every light in the town was extinguished, the last globe raised and the last wick snuffed, Wally would still be sitting in his front parlor, watching out the window.

Not that anyone knew of his vigil, because they didn't. It was generally thought that Wally retired early with Mrs Bristol. However, after the lamps were all put out and after his spouse had retired, Wally stayed up late with only the dull glow of his corncob pipe to give evidence that he was there watching. He owned the small cottage directly across from the Purple County jail and town hall; that is, he owned it with the help of a small mortgage, which he conscientiously tried to reduce.

His salary was not sufficient to do this so he

171

relied on reward money whenever it was available. Then, he was paid mileage by the town for use of his horse, and he had found that by this means he could get a little extra money now and then, although he had to furnish and feed his own horses. Fortunately the mileage figure was a comfortable one and it was difficult to check how many miles a sheriff followed a suspect through the hills, gulches and canyons that rimmed the Purple Valley.

As Wally rocked in his chair he watched the jail closely. There were no prisoners inside but like many another, Wally Bristol carried his work home with him, and it was all stored within his head in neat and orderly fashion. When he sat down in the rocker and smoked his pipe he extracted this or that worry from his mental inventory and went to work on it with his thoughts.

When he could go no further with one particular problem he would wedge it back into its place, take out another and go to work on it, puffing and rocking and watching the jail with his wrinkled, sharp old eyes.

This evening he was thinking about Silver Cloud and the worries that it had brought him. This wasn't the first night he had wrestled with the problem of the silver stallion; he had spent many an hour rocking and puffing and watching and thinking about Jim Walker and the horse.

Walker represented a hundred dollars, dead

or alive. This would be a substantial payment on his mortgage on the little cottage. However, he liked the boy. Still, a hundred dollars was a hundred dollars, and if he planked that down against his principal debt he would have an easy, worryless winter ahead of him. Besides, there was no way to shift the hundred dollars onto the head of Bart Dodge, whom he did not like and on whom he would far rather have collected.

He really didn't believe Walker had killed the man named Sam Parker. Now, Parker there, was a far different story: the sheriff's detective work had brought him the story that Parker had been a petty outlaw from Star Valley.

That Walker had been a member of Butch Cassidy's Wild Bunch at one time he did not doubt, although here his detective work had drawn a blank. Apparently Walker wasn't wanted by any of the Wyoming law officers, but he was well-known among the outlaws of that state and he was regarded as a fast gun. Across the way, a shadow darted from the covert of the black alley next to the jail and stealthily crept along the board walk to the jail entrance.

Wally sat forward slowly and put his leathery hand over the glowing bowl of his pipe. The figure in the shadow of the veranda stopped by the bulletin board where Bristol posted messages of local importance. The figure tacked a small square of white to the board and then, glancing around as if to make sure no one had seen him, the slight figure disappeared into the alley as quickly as it had come.

Wally sat back and grunted, rubbing the smooth walnut handle of his Colt, on the table beside him. Now, he wondered, what was this stunt? What did it mean? He closed his eyes tightly and mentally conjured up the image he had seen, just a darting shadow really, but a familiar figure, nevertheless. Who did he know that looked like a cat, on tiptoe, almost?

He felt he had the identity on the tip of his tongue, but he put it from his mind in the belief that it would come to him quicker that way. He knocked the dottle of his pipe into the tray and repacked it with fresh tobacco from his pouch. He struck a match along the rough seam of his trousers, sucked the flame down deep among the grains, then snuffed the match and hid the glow from the bowl by clamping his palm over its top.

He hated the thought of going on Walker's trail; he hated it even more since he had heard the story going around about Walker having been burned out. That would mean a trip up the valley to investigate the scene. And that would be mileage, of course; ten cents a mile wasn't much but he could go over to Dodge's and ask some questions. And he could stop other places, too.

Then there was the mess about the damn

horse. It was gone now, and he wondered if a suspected murderer would expect him to hunt for the horse. There wasn't much doubt about where the horse was; his first guess would be Dodge's barn, his second guess would be Dodge's corral, and his third would be the horse herd at the Pitchfork. And, if he had to make a fourth choice, it would be one of Dodge's line shacks, and so on. But Dodge would surely be involved somehow.

One thing he didn't like about Dodge was the way the man leaned on the law like a desperately needed crutch when he found it expedient. Other times he avoided legal procedure like a plague, settling things in his own way. Wally chuckled when he thought about Bart Dodge making the statement about giving the horse to Walker if the rancher was tough enough to ride him. Then he chuckled again at the way the young feller had done it, and had enough sand to hold on to the horse in the face of everything Dodge could fight him with. It even looked like Walker was going to take Sally Ackerman away from Bart Dodge. Bart certainly had had the inside track with her until the deal with the horse.

Wally sat up and blinked. A second form was now creeping silently through the night toward his bulletin board at the jail. The solitary figure, a more bulky shape this time, paused at the bulletin board, tacked a second message there,

175

then turned and slowly made his way along the wall.

Wally Bristol went to rocking again and grunted as he had before. So two people had pinned messages to his bulletin board on this night of nights. This was getting to be an interesting problem.

He heard the unmistakable sound of a horse being ridden from the scene. He wondered about the notices; obviously each man didn't want to be seen by any living soul in town. Obviously, too, it was too dark for the second man to read the first man's message and each one had been eager to creep from the scene of his work.

A half-hour passed and Wally believed that the bulletins were all posted for the night. He arose stealthily from his chair and made his way to the door. With his long Colt in one hand he opened the door a crack and looked up and down the street. The cool night air poured in and refreshed him. He went into the street and up the jail steps and paused at the bulletin board. As he was familiar with the other postings, he had no difficulty in locating the two mystery messages. He pulled them from the board and went back across the street walking with quick, catlike steps in his stocking feet.

Back in the house he sat at the small desk in the corner, where he sometimes did paper work

176

at home, and lighted the candle. One by one he smoothed out the papers and read the messages. He found that the slightly built man had left this notice:

CITIZENS OF PURPLE:
JIM WALKER INTENDS TO ROB THE BANK OF PURPLE.

A FRIEND.

The first notice was smoothed out over the second one, the one left by the second, bulkier man. He lifted the paper and read the second message:

RESIDENTS OF PURPLE & SHERIFF BRISTOL:
BART DODGE HAS A PLAN TO ROB THE PURPLE BANK.

IN THE KNOW

Wally Bristol frowned and blew out the candle. He went back to his chair and started puffing his pipe once more. He rocked for some time before he got up and went back to the desk and relighted the single candle. Taking a clean sheet of paper from the drawer he began to print in his slow, painstaking manner:

DEAR BANK ROBBERS:
WHICHEVER OF YOU IT REALLY IS—WATCH OUT.

A FRIEND OF 'IN THE KNOW.'

He regarded his work for some time, chuckling at it and the fact that no one else in Purple had seen the other notes. He sat biting the tip of the pen and thinking and then on a second clean sheet of paper he wrote out the following notice:

NOTICE.

BY THE AUTHORITY VESTED IN ME AS SHERIFF OF PURPLE COUNTY THE FOLLOWING REWARDS ARE NOW EFFECTIVE:

$100 REWARD FOR THE ARREST OF ANY BANK ROBBER.

$100 REWARD FOR INFORMATION AND CAPTURE OF THE THIEVES OF THE HORSE, SILVER CLOUD.

$100 REWARD FOR THE CAPTURE OF THOSE WHO BURNED THE WALKER RANCH.

$100 REWARD FOR THE KILLER OF SAM PARKER.

$100 REWARD FOR PERSONS CAUGHT POSTING ILLEGAL BULLETINS LIABLE TO INCITE RIOT OR A RUN ON THE BANK.

NOTE: ANYONE WISHING TO DOUBLE THESE REWARDS OUT OF CIVIC SPIRIT IS HEREBY AUTHORIZED TO DO SO.

WALLY BRISTOL,
SHERIFF, PURPLE COUNTY.

Wally Bristol sat a while and contemplated what he could do to his principal balance with the five hundred dollars the rewards amounted to, then he stole across the street, still in his stocking feet, and posted the two messages he himself had written. The others he destroyed. As he climbed into bed, he felt better about the situation and he was glad he had stayed up late. He slept soundly.

Morning came and as usual Wally Bristol was one of the first to tromp through the thick ankle-deep dust that comprised the paving of Purple's main street. He opened the sheriff's office and then walked diagonally across the street to the restaurant where he bought breakfast and yesterday's newspaper, which he got for half-price each morning from the restaurant owner. Then he came out of the restaurant as he always did, the paper under his arm and a sliver of wood between his lips as a toothpick.

He moved a battered porch chair into the early morning sun and parked his feet on the rail of the jail veranda. Across the street Mrs Bristol came to the door and shook a rug, making audible comment about somebody always tracking in a load of dirt.

Bristol waved to his spouse and opened the paper before his face thus shutting out the dull, tranquil scene of Purple, and read the news of

179

the world.

By ten o'clock he had read the section through no less than three times. Then one of the Pitchfork cowhands came sauntering casually along the board walk toward the jail. Wally folded his paper and regarded the approaching man. This was a departure from his regular routine because he never looked at anyone directly as a rule but preferred to observe from the covert of his paper. On this particular morning, however, he wanted to miss no detail of facial expression.

'Howdy, Clem,' he greeted.

'Mawnin', Sheriff,' acknowledged the other.

'Lookin' for somethin', Clem?'

'Why, no—just wanted to see what was posted on the board, is all,' declared Clem.

Bristol scowled at the man. 'I don't remember seein' you look at it before.'

'Oh, I looked at it before, Sheriff.'

'When?' The question was sharp and abrupt.

'Why—I dunno—but I did look at it—'

'Well, all right, Clem. For a minute there I wasn't gonna let you look at it, 'cause you never showed no interest before this but if what you say is true, then go ahead and look. Them that show an interest are entitled to look.' Bristol pretended to read his paper.

Clem stared spellbound at the two new notices. Then he turned slowly. 'Man, them's a funny lot o' rewards you got posted, Sheriff.

That all the notices you got, eh?'

'That's the sum total of them,' grumbled Wally from behind the paper. He watched from behind the edge of his paper as the Pitchfork rider got on his horse and left the town by the valley road.

A half hour later Wally was not surprised to see old Dan Ackerman pull up on his buckboard. Ackerman tied the reins around the whip socket, got down and stretched his legs. He stared at Bristol, then he rubbed his hands across his buttocks to take away the soreness brought on by the hard board seat.

'Howdy, you old sidewinder,' greeted Ackerman.

'Howdy, yourself, you dried-up, ornery prune,' answered Bristol, lowering the paper. Ackerman came up the steps, then turned his back on Bristol and looked at the board.

'What's new?' asked Ackerman. He searched the messages quickly, going from one to another and finally coming back to the one on rewards.

'Nuthin's new, Ackerman. How come you're lookin' at my bulletin board?'

'Why, it's a public board, ain't it? I pay taxes, don't I?' Ackerman whirled on the sheriff.

'Well, you pay taxes—late. But I guess that don't mean you gotta read the board late. What you lookin' for?'

181

'Why, I was just standin' here, gettin' the kinks out, yuh ol' reprobate. How come yo're so sassy and full o' greens an' vinegar this mornin'?'

'I didn't know you could read,' laughed Wally.

Ackerman turned to the board; he was rereading the message on rewards and shaking his head as he memorized each line.

'You want I should make a copy of that so that you can take it to whoever yo're memorizing it for?' asked Bristol.

Ackerman jumped. 'I can remember what I read, Bristol. Not that I was tryin' to remember; I was just marvelin' at the waste of money we tax-payers got to put up with. What this county needs is a ridin', shootin' sheriff that goes out trackin', not a blamed edjicated note-writer!'

Ackerman strode off down the boardwalk, first taking one more quick look at the two posted messages. Bristol went back to his newspaper, but not to reread it. He was thinking about Bart Dodge and Jim Walker, and wondering if anyone really would try to rob the bank.

As he sat and read he made careful note of the fact that every other person in Purple who read the notices became excited, whereas the first two readers had been quite calm.

182

CHAPTER NINETEEN

Mold Dillon had crossed the Purple range as he had promised. And now, as he sat in Bart Dodge's partially burned-out ranch house, he was nervous with the excitement of the coming job. Mold got his name from his classic technique of running a soap mold around the crack of a safe. With a little nitro packed in the mold he could open a heavy safe as gently as he could a woman's purse. He worked for a flat amount; the amount in the safe meant nothing to him. To Mold, a fee in the hand was worth a good deal more than a fortune in the iron box, and for that reason he worked for five thousand dollars, paid in advance.

However, this deal was not for cash but cows, and five hundred head of Dodge's herd had been rolled on their sides by sweating cowboys and branded with the Pitchfork on the opposite flank and then rerolled and branded with Mold's own brand of the Coffeepot that he ran in Brown's Hole, Wyoming. The job had taken some time with the necessity of branding each cow twice in the accepted manner of changing ownership, and it was now late in the week.

Dodge easily explained the sale as an attempt to recoup from the disastrous fire that had left him short on everything but cows and running stock. The neighbors accepted it as logical. Finally the last of the five hundred head were run up to the far end of the valley where Mold's riders drove them toward the rail spur, miles away.

With the settling of the other details, Dodge now cursed two mysteries he couldn't explain. One was the strange message on the sheriff's bulletin board, news of which had been brought in by Clem. Dodge had questioned the thick-witted rider a dozen times before sending a second rider in, only to have him come back and verify Clem's version of the bulletins. The second thing was the strange fact that Lash Wade had never returned from Brown's Hole, Wyoming, and Mold Dillon was the last person who had seen him. Bart feared that the two things were related but he didn't see how they could be—unless Walker, who he was sure had fired his ranch, had intercepted Wade and killed him.

Now with Wade gone, things were running badly. Briggs, a fast hand with a gun and eager to kill, was not a good foreman; he was competent at sneaking around in the dark and doing dirty work, but his usefulness ended there. He did not have the respect of the men, although they were afraid of him; they knew he didn't know ranching and they could get away with loafing without his knowing it.

As soon as Mold's men had taken over the

cattle, Bart let a large portion of his own hands go. He kept a few at the ranch as a blind, but actually he had made up his mind not to stay in the valley. He would move on and assume a new name after the bank robbery. He would never see the punchers that he would leave on Pitchfork, and they in turn would never see their back wages. He had kept on those faithful few who had been working only for found with the promise that their back pay would be met when things took an up-turn.

It was Saturday night and the long shadows of the Purple Mountains were beginning to fill the valley. The plan was to hit the bank around two in the morning when the town was quiet. This was likely even though it was Saturday, as most of the ranchers met their payroll on the following week at the end of the month; most of the cowboys would be too broke to come to town.

Mold had his black satchel packed and on the table; he had gone over the intricate and deadly items a score of times to make sure that nothing would go wrong during the final hour. The soap had been twice strained for it had to be absolutely pure; a single bubble could hold back the deadly nitroglycerine from finding the weak points of lock and hinges. Mold sat in his chair and calmly smoked a long, black cigar; from time to time he knocked the ash off against the black bag containing the

185

nitroglycerine. Dodge was getting dressed and packing a carpet bag; he was traveling light and selecting with care what he would take.

A spare gun went into the bag, a small custom-sized Colt, a spaying knife and other items. He glanced up as Briggs forked his horse into the yard at great speed and burst into the room with a wide-eyed expression of incredulity on his face.

'I told you to bring the stallion. Where's Silver Cloud?' asked Bart. He was annoyed with Briggs for, despite his skill with a gun, he always seemed to fail at the simplest things, like posting the note on the town bulletin board the other night.

'I did what you said,' began Briggs, irritated by Dodge's surly manner and the way the rancher was looking at him. 'I went down and I got the stallion at sunset, then I took him to the crick and started to wash off the water paint.'

'Get to the point, you fool! What about it?'

'That paint won't come off,' complained Briggs. 'I scrubbed and I scrubbed, but if you ask me that's a black hoss you got and no silver stallion.'

'For Gawd's sake, that paint has got to come off—that's part of the plan!' yelled Bart.

'There's somethin' else about that hoss,' said Briggs.

'I suppose we used the wrong paint,' moaned Bart.

'No, that hoss has got a Window-Sash brand on his flank!'

'What?' yelped Dodge.

'That's right,' laughed Briggs, suddenly seeing something funny about it.

'Stop laughing, you damn hyena, and let me think. By Gawd, do you see what happened? Walker slipped in here and got that painted silver horse and left one of Weaver's horses in its place. That wouldn't be any trick for a horse thief like him!'

'Does this mean that the hoist is off?' asked Mold, looking up. He was amused that for once he had a better than average deal going for himself. He had five hundred head of Dodge's cattle headed for Brown's Hole, the best of the bunch, and those that were left were starving to death. If Dodge wanted them back now, he would have to pay for Mold's trouble and the price wouldn't be cheap. Mold thought two hundred and fifty cows would be about right.

'No—the job comes off. The horse being gone don't make all that difference. We still have Walker's gear that we can drop along the trail on the way to the railroad—the things we took from the shack before you burned it.'

'Let's get started, then. I don't like to stall when a job's ready,' Mold declared. He stood up, clasping his bag, and walked to the door.

The three rode away from the ranch, allegedly to accompany Dillon to Purple where he would leave to overtake his cattle. Their departure was innocent enough and none noticed the small bag that Bart carried on the far side of his horse. There was one exception, however, and that rider dogged their trail, keeping to the rear as they passed up the valley. Soon it was dark and nothing was heard except the steady pelting of their horses' hoofs and the occasional jingle and rattle of harness.

★　　★　　★

Wally Bristol had not yet blown out the lamp. Mrs Bristol had long since gone to bed and had left him sitting quietly in the parlor, rocking and smoking as always. Wally was smiling as he took from his pocket a folded envelope and regarded it as he rocked. Slowly he unfolded it and smoothed it across his knee. It was addressed to him and was postmarked from a Wyoming town. Slowly, he once more opened the envelope and extracted the letter. He read it through again:

Wally Bristol, Sheriff of Purple County.
Dear Wally:
This will let you know that I have left Purple Valley on the advice of my friend Jim Walker. This letter will be proof that Jim Walker is innocent of killing Sam Parker. Craig Briggs did this job for Bart Dodge.

Bart planned the stealing of Silver Cloud at the haying dance, then he planned to rob the Bank of Purple and hang the job on Jim by using the stallion and some of Jim's things. Jim Walker is a square dealer and he never did a bad thing. I am writing this letter for old Jim in the hope that you will let him off with a short prison sentence if you ever are lucky enouf to ketch him, which I doubt. I swear that the above is writ by me and true as the Gospel.

James Whitmore (Lash) Wade
Alias Jake Wade

Wally sighed and refolded the letter. He raised the globe on the lamp near his chair and blew out the flame. He continued to rock in the darkness. If this letter was legal proof, then three-fifths of the rewards posted were his. The remaining forty per cent was his if he could apprehend the robbers when they tried to crack the bank.

He had passed the notice off as a joke, chiefly to allay the fears of Bank President Finly and Morton, the storekeeper, who was one of the heavier depositors. He certainly didn't intend to split the reward with anyone, so he maintained a lonely vigil each night.

To do this it was only necessary to shift his chair slightly before the window. From the new spot he could watch two sides of the bank much the same as he had watched the jail next door for years. Every night he had watched and waited and still they had not come, and now he began to doubt if they really would try to rob the bank.

Twice a night he crept out—once at one-thirty and once at four-thirty—to steal a glance at the two sides he could not see. Then, too, he relied on his hearing to give him some clue. The shades in the bank windows were always kept raised, and the robbers would have to work in the burglar light or pull the shades. If they tried the latter, Wally could tell by the reflection in the windows that the shades were drawn.

He made the journey at one-thirty and the coolness of the night air refreshed him, although he was extremely tired after four days of watching. Nothing was stirring, either in the town or around the bank. He went back to the rocking chair and rocked and smoked.

He felt his head begin to nod and he fought off the drowsy feeling. He had good reason to suspect that this was the particular night. He had had the news of Pitchfork's burning, and if Dodge was really going to move against the bank he would have to do it soon, for the fire had forced him to sell what good stock he still owned.

The sheriff jumped, blinking, suddenly realizing that in a moment of exhaustion he had closed his eyes. He decided to go to the kitchen and pump some water to refresh himself. But first, however, as long as he was decided on such a drastic move as to dash cold spring water into his face, he could enjoy the incomparable luxury of shutting his eyes for a full two minutes. Ah, what luxury this was! There was nothing so heavenly as to let the weary lids come down over his tired and burning eyes. He snuggled into the confines of his rocker and pulled the blanket from the back down around his shoulders. But only for the space of a moment would he do this, then he would bound into the kitchen and douse himself with the spring water. After all, no one could rob the Bank of Purple in five minutes. Then Wally Bristol made his second mistake of the evening; he fell sound asleep. The chime clock behind him struck the familiar tones that he never heard; it was two o'clock in the morning.

Wally dreamed. He dreamed that he was in the kitchen and that he was vigorously pumping the handle of the small pump. The cool water was splashing on the nape of his neck and reviving him wonderfully. Then he awoke and found it was no dream. He was still in his rocker but there was something cool and cold against his neck; he blinked and thought about it for a moment but without much thinking he decided that it was the cold, round muzzle of a revolver.

When he heard the breathing, he knew that someone was holding a Colt .45 against the back of his neck. Wally felt his scalp go prickly with fear. He cursed himself for not locking his back door. Now someone, perhaps the bank robber, had snuck in and got the drop on him.

'That you, Dodge?' he asked in a whisper. He had no desire to awaken his wife.

'No,' came the muffled answer.

'Oh, Craig Briggs, come to do the dirty work, eh?'

'Wrong ag'in, Wally; it's me—Jim Walker. I come to help you.'

'Come to help me die, eh, Walker?'

'Don't be silly, Bristol. We've a good chance of taking them without a fight if we play it right.'

Wally tried to roll his eyes around, without moving his head, to see the other man.

'How do you throw your voice like that, Walker?'

'What you mean, Wally?'

'Your voice is coming from the window, but I can feel where your Colt is nudgin' my neck,' said Bristol, his tone tense and irritated.

He heard footsteps behind him.

'Why there ain't no Colt against your neck, Wally. It's just the concho on this blanket of yours—it's caught inside your collar. We better hurry—they been in the bank a few minutes already!'

Jim stepped to the door and Wally frantically pulled on his boots, saying nothing more. He rushed to Walker's side and they both stared across at the bank.

CHAPTER TWENTY

The street was quiet. Only the soft, silver light of the stars came down to illuminate it, with all the buildings casting dark shadows into the dusty street. From somewhere nearby they heard a horse whicker shortly as though someone had suddenly clamped a cautious hand over its muzzle. The finely pulverized dust of the street was dimpled by human feet and horses' hoofs, and in the light of the stars it looked like the surface of a sandy desert: lonely, forlorn and dry. The whole country needed rain, and in the valley the grass was brittle and crackling underfoot.

Walker looked out at the street, so still and quiet. He wondered if he'd be standing here now, about to intercept a bank robbery if the summer had not been so dry. He never would have come to Purple that day he won the silver stallion on Dodge's silly statement if his animals hadn't gone through his supply of salt. Dodge would never have been so desperate as to try and rob the bank if it had not been for the dry spell.

He stepped onto the porch with Wally Bristol at his side. They stared at the bank. The burglar light was burning dimly, but no shadow stirred in the windows.

'I don't see nothin',' declared Wally. 'You sure they went in there?'

'They pried some of those flimsy bars off the side window, and they're inside now,' answered Walker, straining his eyes toward the windows.

'If they're in there, they must be plastered to the floor like a wet newspaper,' said Wally.

'Look at that!' Jim said.

'What? Where? Look at what?'

'On the bank ceiling, see that little shadow moving.'

'That's the waves in the glass window doin' that, Walker. I seen it a million times before this.'

'All right, maybe it is, but I thought I saw something moving just the same. Let's go over there and peek in the front window.'

They tiptoed across the street with their guns drawn and dropped into the deep dust before the horse trough outside the bank. Cautiously they raised their heads above the window sill level and peered in. Wally Bristol cursed unbelievingly.

For twenty years he had been sheriff of Purple. In all that time no single business establishment had ever been robbed, let alone the bank. Before that time—and Wally could remember the peaceful tenure of the former political appointee—nothing in the town had ever been robbed. Never even had a horse been stolen in this community where no other means of travel existed.

And while every form of strife and trouble had been known in Purple Valley, precious little had ever happened in the town itself. That was why, as Bristol stared into the back of the well-lighted bank, he couldn't believe his eyes at the tableau disclosed there.

In the single light of the burglar lamp, the immense black front of the locked safe was the back-drop for a large portion of the rear of the room. Against it, was the silver-gray head of Mold Dillon as he worked with his bare head close to the safe doors.

Standing fully erect, looking as bold as a wolf in a pen of sheep, was Bart Dodge. He was heavily armed with one revolver swung about his waist in a holster and another bulging his coat beneath his left arm. He was dressed for fast travel with a pair of fancy dark-brown Eastern riding pants and shiny brown boots. His shirt was a deep navy blue and his vest of soft doeskin. His hat was the color of buckskin and it went well with the vest. As Walker stared open-mouthed at the boldness of the bank robber, he thought it was too bad such a handsome man had to be a thief.

It came to him like a flash then. He remembered thinking the same thing some years before when Dodge, at the time a thinner version of his present self, had been the inside man on one of Butch Cassidy's jobs. At last he knew where Dodge knew him from, and he marveled that had it not been for watching him through the window tonight, Dodge's identity probably always would have puzzled Jim.

Now Dodge went to the open window. For a second Wally and Jim had a brief glimpse of the pockmarked features of Briggs as the little crook said something to the boss. Dodge pointed with his hand toward the front of the building with all the poise and aplomb of one directing a traveler, and Wally and Jim dropped flat in the shadows behind the horse trough. They could hear the stealthy footsteps coming slowly around the building.

Walker wedged himself flat against the trough, but it was too short for his length and his head poked around one end. Jim could see Briggs as he came around the corner. The small crook stood around five feet four and his rounded features were heavily pockmarked so that in the moonlight his complexion appeared mottled. He wore high-heeled boots to give him more height but now they were sunk in the dust of the street. He brushed back his hat and looked around.

Briggs stared hard at the sheriff's darkened

house and then turned and looked up and down the street. Still he didn't appear satisfied. He reached down and eased his revolver out of the tied-down holster, spun the weapon around on his finger in a confident gesture and dropped it back into leather. Apparently satisfied, he turned to go.

Walker came up then and made a rush for the man. Briggs spun halfway around, his expression a picture of surprise, fear and rage. He drew his gun with one hand as he grabbed for the charging Walker with the other. Jim knew he must be quick, and the panther-like strength of the killer surprised him. Walker drove his head into Briggs' face and he heard the muffled gasp of the other, apparently reluctant to cry out for fear of arousing the townsmen.

Jim felt his skull strike Briggs' nose and mouth and felt the man's teeth cut into his forehead. Blood was spouting from Briggs' nose and mouth from the butting. Jim now stepped in close and grabbed the other's gun wrist in both hands. He twisted the forearm sharply. There was a crunching sound as the bone broke and the gun dropped to the ground.

Jim grasped the outlaw's sagging form and cracked him in the jaw with a solid balled fist. Unconscious, the outlaw slipped to the ground where he lay like a pile of old clothes.

Wally Bristol's agile form darted silently, his

fist grasping a cocked Colt. The lawman made a dash for the three horses that were starting to spook at the noise and the scent of blood.

Bristol was among the wild-eyed horses in an instant, and with a pat here and a word there he had them quiet as Jim crept to a position beneath the window.

Inside Dodge had heard the horses snort and stamp. As Briggs had not reported back from his inspection of the street, the outlaw glanced significantly at Mold Dillon who looked up from his work with the nitro for a second and then went back to his task. Dodge hastened to the window where he looked out. He saw the small form of Wally Bristol among the horses but he mistakenly thought the lawman was the diminutive Briggs and in a harsh whisper he called for quiet.

'Damn fool, can't even watch the horses,' he commented to Dillon.

Jim jumped up in the opening of the window and pointed his pistol inside. 'Hands up, Dodge, and don't move!' he yelled, shattering the stillness of the town.

Dodge whirled around, his face twisted with fury. But as Walker stood looking he realized they were too late. Mold Dillon was rushing for the front of the bank and the fuse even now was hissing toward the soap mold on the safe door. Jim dropped to the ground, covering his face and yelling for Bristol to take cover.

Then it happened. A horrendous explosion shook the bank, causing the other buildings in the town to tremble. Dust began to settle as things were still clattering to the floor within the bank building. Here and there lamps winked alive in windows as the curious townsfolk came awake to see what had shattered the night's serenity.

Jim jumped to the window once more but the room was dark, with the light extinguished by the blast. Orange lances of flame stabbed at him from the darkness as he stood silhouetted in the light of the window. He heard the slugs pick at the wood but his own shots blasted back through the dust-filled, debris-cluttered room. A form leaped up and dashed through the window with a crash of broken glass and fell onto the board sidewalk. Then the man was up and running again. Jim recognized Bart Dodge heading across the street.

Jim leaped into the building while behind him he could hear Wally Bristol caught in the tangle of horses, trying to calm them down. Wally dared not step back from the reins he clutched as the three scared horses alternately lunged skyward.

Walker tripped over something and the force of the blow cutting across his shin told him he had stumbled on the safe door that now reposed on the floor. Now a second form leaped up against the space of the broken front window, and Jim saw Mold Dillon's portly shape scamper out to the street and safety.

Jim was up and through the window next and a sudden rumbling noise made him turn and look at the bank, the target of Dillon's chemistry. He stumbled along the board walk and tried a shot at Dillon but the safe-cracker was hotfooting it down the street with such a comical gait that Jim was thankful he missed. No one in the valley ever saw Mold Dillon again that night, or afterward for that matter, and some said he must have run all the way back to Wyoming.

Across the street Jim heard the excited, shrill whicker of Silver Cloud and in an instant he knew what was happening. Dodge, running for his life, had stumbled on the stallion when he had cut for cover behind Bristol's house. Now the crook was going to make good his escape on Cloud's back, and there was no horse that could come close to catching the silver stallion.

Jim raced for Bristol's house. Into the yard he came just as Dodge fought his way into the saddle and lashed the horse down through the back yards toward the valley road and safety. Walker leveled his pistol and started to fire, but he couldn't press the trigger for fear of hitting the horse. He dropped the weapon to his side with a curse.

Then luck, which had never been kind to Walker, played a card. A cry came from Dodge as he seemed to be plucked backward from the saddle. For the fraction of an instant he hung in the air as if by magic, then spun around in a wonderful somersault that made Walker cry out in amazement. Walker raced forward, not knowing what had happened. Near the house a ghostly, white-clad apparition danced excitedly up and down. As Jim ran closer he laughed with joy; Dodge had caught himself on a stout clothesline, and the ghost was only a stiff suit of underwear hanging near the house and bounding up and down as the taut line still quivered.

As Walker grabbed the outlaw rancher and dragged him up, he found that there was no fight in Dodge. The wind had been knocked from his body and even his pistols had jarred out of the holsters in the freak capture. Walker felt the clothesline for a second and he made up his mind he would own it someday. The line was stout and it was a wonder that Dodge hadn't torn himself in half as he had galloped away, until plucked so suddenly from the saddle.

Jim shoved the outlaw before him and they headed across the street where Wally Bristol held Craig Briggs by the scruff of the neck and a group of citizens with swinging lanterns had gathered. Jim glanced up and found that daylight had come in an instant; then he saw the lightning and heard the thunder—the rumble he had heard moments before.

Rain burst down in torrents as the clouds swept up from the valley and closed out all the dawn-lighted sky. Even as they crossed the street the dust turned to mud. When they crowded into the musty office of Wally Bristol the place was jammed to the walls with people in their hastily donned clothing.

The faces around him were smiling and laughing as he pushed Dodge ahead. Hands reached out to slap him on the back. Jim Walker had never seen people look at him like this; suddenly he was a hero—he had saved their money from the robbers, and for that they were willing to forget everything they had ever disliked about him. Dodge was thrust behind bars and he turned and snarled at the men as they crowded before the cell. He ranted and raved and cursed them with every invective at his command. The citizens stood spellbound as his bitter, true nature revealed itself.

Walker shook a few hands but quickly left them all to find the stallion and start the long ride down Purple Valley. Later, when he rode into the yard at Ackerman's, the rain still came down in torrents. He rode straight to the barn and put the stallion inside. As Jim fondly rubbed down Silver Cloud, he knew that—regardless of everything that had been said—the horse was good luck. He turned toward the house, and in the window he saw

Sally waiting and watching. As he crossed the yard it continued to rain just as hard but the sun shone brightly for a moment above the Purple Mountains and Jim saw a large multi-colored rainbow. He laughed and pointed to it and the girl in the window nodded her head before she left to open the door for the man she loved.